KNIGHT TIME

A TANNER NOVEL - BOOK 29

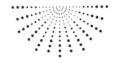

REMINGTON KANE

YEAR ZERO
PUBLISHING, LLC

INTRODUCTION

KNIGHT TIME – A TANNER NOVEL – BOOK 29

Tanner reunites with Henry Knight after Henry, now fifteen, needs his help.

The stakes are high, and the authorities are involved. The police and the FBI have to play by the rules, Tanner doesn't. And he plays in a whole other league.

ACKNOWLEDGMENTS

I write for you.

—Remington Kane

PROLOGUE

OUTSIDE PITTSBURGH, PENNSYLVANIA, FIVE YEARS EARLIER

WHILE OUT TO FULFILL A CONTRACT ON A UKRAINIAN mobster named Kyril Yatsenko, Tanner and Sara met a ten-year-old boy named Henry Knight. He was an inquisitive kid and smart. After viewing the sophisticated sniper rifle Tanner was carrying, Henry knew he wasn't out in the woods hunting deer.

"You're a secret agent, aren't you?"

"Something like that," Tanner said.

"I'm gonna call you Agent X."

Tanner and Sara walked Henry home and learned that he had lost his mother to violence. A neighbor, Boyd Kessler, had killed Henry's mother and gotten away with the murder thanks to a false alibi given by a friend of Kessler's under threat of violence. The alibi witness was later slain in what appeared to be a violent mugging. In actuality, Kessler had killed the man because he was threatening to go back on his story.

As young as he was, Henry had sought to kill Kessler for what he'd done. He had failed, and Kessler wasn't above murdering a child in order to seek revenge.

After dropping Henry off at home, Sara and Tanner headed back to the location where the target would be. Henry followed along and remained undetected until it was too late. He stayed by Sara's side while Tanner moved in to fulfill his contract.

Tanner met strong resistance in the form of Yatsenko's gang. While he was dealing with them, Yatsenko managed to slip out amid a group of prostitutes while wearing a disguise.

Sara and Henry had waited for Tanner at the rendezvous point where they had left their car. After hearing the sounds of a firefight and an explosion, Tanner had yet to appear. Henry grew worried for him.

"Where's Agent X?" Henry asked. "I thought you said he would meet us at the car."

"He'll be here, honey. Nothing stops Agent X."

Henry smiled up at her. "You like him, don't you?"

"I… yes, I guess I do, but let that be our little secret, okay?"

"Okay," Henry said, as a sound reached his sensitive ears. Someone was running toward them along an old deer trail. Henry released Sara's hand and spun around.

A homely-looking woman was pointing a gun at Sara, she wore heavy makeup, a dress, and a pair of red spiked heels.

Henry, who as far as Sara could tell was devoid of fear, walked over to the woman, reached up, and yanked off the wig.

"It's a guy in a dress, and he's wearing makeup too. Ugh, gross."

It was Yatsenko. He snatched the wig back from Henry and shoved him toward the car, while speaking in his strong Slavic accent.

"Come on, little boy, you and I are going for a ride."

Despite the gun pointed at her face and the danger it posed to herself and Henry, Sara took the time to puzzle over the heels. She knew several women who had trouble keeping their balance in high heels, and yet, Yatsenko was walking just fine, and he had even traversed the uneven terrain of the forest deer path. Looking closer, Sara saw that

Yatsenko's calves were smooth, as if they were shaved on a regular basis.

Yatsenko narrowed his eyes as he saw where she was looking. "What?"

"Nothing," Sara said, but the corners of her mouth curled up in a knowing smile.

"Slowly unsling that rifle and hand over the gun. If you attempt to shoot me, I'll kill the boy."

"No, you won't," said a voice from the top of the embankment. When Sara turned her head to look, she saw Tanner clad in full body armor, as he held a large revolver extended and steadied by both hands. The weapon was a Taurus Judge. The Taurus was a monster of a revolver that could fire either .45 Colt cartridges or .410 shells. Tanner had loaded his with .410 shotgun shells.

Henry cried out, "Agent X!" and Sara reached over and yanked the boy away from Yatsenko.

With Henry in the clear, Tanner fired twice and sent triple-ought buckshot into Yatsenko's rather buxom bosom. Unfortunately for Yatsenko, the box of tissues he had stuffed inside his bra did nothing to stop the massive pellets from devastating his heart and lungs. After hitting the ground, Yatsenko let out a long wheezing sigh, then breathed no more.

"Wow!" Henry said, as he moved over to stare down at Yatsenko.

Sara attempted to hold Henry back from the

body, but the boy was insistent upon getting a closer look. Sara let him, and after picking up Yatsenko's gun, she walked over to greet Tanner. She had noticed the odd way he was holding his head, as well as the numerous dings on the body armor.

"Are you all right?"

"I'll heal, but let's get out of here. I heard sirens in the distance as I was walking away from the house."

"We need to take Henry with us."

"Why?"

"He's seen a lot, Tanner; he needs us to explain things to him."

Tanner looked over at Henry, who was still gazing down at Yatsenko's fresh corpse with stark fascination.

Sara urged Henry to get in the car, and after Tanner removed his body armor, he tossed the components in the vehicle's trunk, along with the empty M249 he'd been using. Before climbing in the car, he also changed his pants and grabbed a sweatshirt, since the old clothing was speckled with blood on the sleeves and cuffs.

As Tanner sat next to Sara, he winced at the feel of the seat against his back and leaned forward. Sara reached over and lifted his shirt, she then hissed in sympathy at the web of bruises covering his back, as well as his stomach and chest.

"You are going to hurt like hell tomorrow."

"Wrong. It hurts like hell right now."

Sara had placed the car in gear, but she paused in depressing the gas pedal. "Do you need a doctor?"

"I don't think so, but I would love a beer."

Sara laughed with relief and drove back to the highway.

Henry leaned forward and stuck his head between the seats, then stared up at Tanner with a huge grin on his face. "Another successful mission, Agent X?"

Tanner smiled. "Didn't your grandmother ever tell you not to take rides from strangers, kid?"

"You're not strangers. She's Sara, and your name is Tanner, but your code name is Agent X. Who was that man in the dress you shot? He talked funny, was he a foreign spy?"

"Something like that."

"Are you hungry, Henry? We'll stop and get burgers and shakes," Sara said.

"Awesome, but I'd better call my grandma, so she won't get worried."

"We'll do that when we stop to eat."

"Okay, and hey Agent X?"

"What, kid?"

"You sure shot that guy back there."

"You didn't see that, Henry… understand?"

Henry furrowed his brow, but then smiled. "You mean that it's like a government secret?"

"Something similar, and you can't tell anyone what you saw. Do you think you can keep a secret?"

Henry straightened and sent Tanner a salute. "Yes sir, Agent X. You can count on me, sir."

Tanner smiled. "I know I can, Henry. You're a hell of a good kid."

THAT EVENING TANNER WAS LOOKING FORWARD TO going to bed early and sleeping until well past dawn. As he was removing his clothes to shower, he came across a note Henry had given him to read later. When he unfolded it, he saw that it contained two wrinkled dollar bills. Wrapped inside the money was a dime and three pennies.

Tanner read the note, and then he read it again.

He sat atop the closed toilet lid and thought about the words that Henry had written to him. After coming to a decision, Tanner turned on the water and stepped into the shower, but before doing so, he set the alarm on his phone to wake him at three a.m.

He was not going to get much sleep after all.

Tanner followed Kessler to Henry's home that night. Kessler had planned to burn Henry and his family alive in an arson fire.

Boyd Kessler crept over to the side of the house and tried the garage door. It was locked, but the window on the side of the garage slid open. He leaned in and placed the gas can beside a yard tractor. He was lifting his right leg to climb inside when the flat end of a shovel came crashing down on the back of his skull.

Kessler fell while moaning and saw nothing but flashes of light dance before his eyes, as severe pain made him wonder if his head had been split open.

Before he knew it, he was being dragged away by his hair. It should have hurt like hell, but it didn't. The earlier blow had commandeered every pain receptacle in his head, and his skull was already pounding. The misery did nothing to clear his mind and Kessler struggled to remain conscious.

His gangly form slid easily over the cushion of dead leaves, but the occasional rock or tree root sent a prickle of pain along his ribs when he was dragged over them.

Kessler's mind became focused enough for him to open his eyes. He was about to cry out and ask what was happening when he began tumbling end over end.

He came to rest against a tree. That resulted in

the aching in his skull getting competition, as his back screamed at him with a fresh agony all its own. He lay there moaning, bleeding, and searching for a sign of who it was that was beating him like a mongrel mutt.

That was when Kessler saw the figure walking casually down the hill toward him, and from the way he moved, you'd think the man was out for a stroll. It was too dark and shadowy to make out the man's features, but he was holding his head in a funny way, sort of leaning to one side as if his neck hurt.

Then a beam of silvery moonlight fell between the bare branches of the trees and Kessler saw it reflect off the knife the man carried.

"Who the hell are you?"

The only answer Kessler received was a kick to the side of his head, while his last sight was the flash of the knife. That was followed by his final sensation, the exquisite, albeit brief, agony of a punctured heart.

A short time later, his corpse was lifted from the ground, carried several yards, and dumped unceremoniously into a pre-dug grave.

The body would never be found.

As usual, Henry was the first one up in the morning at his house, and he went outside to enjoy the fresh snow that had fallen just before sunrise. Also, there was something he had to check on.

Although his destination was certain, being a boy, Henry meandered before reaching it, and he even gave chase to a snowshoe hare he had spied, but lost sight of the white creature after it burrowed beneath a bush.

Henry sighed. If he had been carrying his rifle his family could have been eating that hare for dinner.

When he finally reached his destination, he stood at the top of the hill that looked down on Kessler's trailer, and was disappointed to see no signs of shoe prints in the snow. He'd been hoping to see a single set of tracks leading in and another set leading out, with the trailer door hanging by one hinge, as if it had been kicked in.

With his shoulders slumping and his head hanging low, Henry walked off and headed for his secret hideout inside a hollow tree.

When he reached it and ducked inside, he was shocked to see that someone had left an envelope for him in the cavity he called his memory hole. The envelope was bigger than the type his grandmother mailed stuff in, and brown too.

It was taped to the inside of the tree and had his

name printed on it. When Henry opened it, he found the note he had given to Tanner.

It read:

Dear Agent X,

I HAVE AN ASSIGNMENT FOR YOU.

I want you to get rid of the bad guy who killed my mom.

I've tried to do it myself but I'm just a kid.

All the money I have is with this note and I know it's not much, but maybe it's enough?

I hope so.

Boyd Kessler scares me, Agent X. Sometimes I think he'll hurt my grandma too.

OK, that's all I had to say, and I hope you'll help.

YOUR FRIEND FOR LIFE,
Henry Knight

HENRY FOLDED THE NOTE AND REALIZED THAT THERE was something else in the envelope.

It was another note, and there was a small plastic baggie attached to it. The clear bag held the four gold teeth of Boyd Kessler.

When Henry saw what the baggie contained, his

mouth dropped open in wonder, and he read the succinct note.

Dear Henry,

MISSION ACCOMPLISHED!

Your friend for life,
    Agent X

Henry slipped everything back in the envelope and placed it in his memory hole, where it rested beside the picture of his mother.

1

MR. POPULAR

STARK, TEXAS, FIVE YEARS LATER

TANNER, WHOSE REAL NAME WAS CODY PARKER, WAS on the western edge of his property checking fences while on horseback. The ranch foreman, Doc, was on vacation with his daughter and granddaughter, so Cody was handling some of Doc's day-to-day duties. If he came across a fence that needed mending, he would have Doc's young assistant Bobby return later to do the work.

The sky was an endless dome of blue with not even a wisp of cloud to mar it. Being winter, the temperature was low despite the bright sunshine. A look of contentment was displayed on Cody's face as he rode. He had spent decades away from the land,

land his family had lived on for generations. Being back on it and raising a family was like a dream come true. For a long time it was a desire he had suppressed, while thinking it to be an impossibility. He had been presumed dead. Resurrecting himself was one of the best moves he had ever made.

His friend Romeo once told him that being Tanner was more of an adventure than a life. Those words had been true. Now Cody had a life, he had a family, and he had reclaimed his identity and his legacy.

His work was almost completed when he spotted the small huddled figure from a quarter mile away. If he hadn't been elevated by riding on horseback, he might not have glimpsed the small form kneeling in a shallow depression that was lower than the terrain surrounding it.

The figure turned out to be a child of no more than three. It was a cold day and the boy was dressed in only a pair of jeans and a sweatshirt. The shirt had the figure of a cartoon moose on it. The moose was smiling; the boy was not. As Cody came closer, the boy reacted by taking glances in his direction, although he never looked directly at Cody.

"Hey kid, what are you doing out here?"

The boy didn't answer. Cody dismounted, removed his jacket, and walked toward the youth, who was shivering from the low temperature. The kid still wouldn't look at him.

"What's your name?"

There was no answer. Cody met resistance at first when he attempted to place his jacket over the boy's shoulders, that ended when the kid felt the warmth of the sheepskin lining. Once he had the jacket fastened around the boy, Cody waved a hand in front of his face. The boy failed to follow the movement.

I think he's autistic, Cody thought. He smiled at the boy. "We'll find your mom and get you back to her, okay, buddy?"

He took out his phone to discover that he didn't have a signal. On the outer areas of the ranch the cell signals were sporadic. Cody lifted the boy up and carried him back to the horse, with a bit of extra effort he managed to climb back into the saddle while cradling the boy in one arm.

He rode slowly toward a road that ran past the ranch. It was seldom used, and he saw no traffic as he neared it. Across the street was the rear of a house that belonged to Barbara Lang. Mrs. Lang had been one of Cody's teachers as he was growing up.

Once there, Cody found that he had a signal and could make a call. He phoned the chief of police, Steve Mendez, who was a good friend.

"Hey Cody, can I call you back? I've got a crisis to deal with here."

"Would that be a missing boy who's about three years old?"

"You've seen him?"

"I've got him. He wandered onto my ranch."

"Is he all right?"

"He's cold but looks okay. He's autistic, isn't he?"

"Yeah, and his name is Jarod. He's Barbara Lang's grandson. Barb had an attack of some kind while she was babysitting him and headed out the door. The boy wandered off on his own while she was incapacitated."

"Is Barbara okay?"

"The doctor I talked to said it looks like she had what they call a mini stroke. It made her pass out. When she came to and saw that Jarod was gone, she almost had a heart attack too. Where are you, Cody? I'll bring the boy's mama to get him."

Cody told Steve where he could be found. The chief arrived four minutes later with Jarod's anxious mother riding beside him in the passenger seat. Following along behind the patrol car was a long line of pickup trucks and cars.

After handing over Jarod to his mother, Cody gestured at the vehicles and spoke to the chief. Mendez was Cody's height but carried more muscle. His dark hair was hidden under the black Stetson he routinely wore. The chief was seldom in uniform. He preferred jeans and kept his badge pinned to his belt in warm weather and on the outside of his jacket when it was cold, as it was on this day.

"What's all this, Steve?"

"I put the word out that we needed volunteers to help look for Jarod. These are the people who had arrived at the station before your call came in."

"The boy is lucky I was out here when I was. He wouldn't have done well in this chill much longer."

Jarod's mother reached out and gave Cody's hand a squeeze. "Thank you for saving my son, Mr. Parker."

Cody tipped the cowboy hat he was wearing. "I'm glad I could help. What's your name?"

"I'm Caroline Lang; I guess you could say we're neighbors. I moved in with my mother-in-law, Barbara, after my husband died."

Cody studied Caroline and guessed that she was maybe twenty-four. She was a beauty with blonde hair and long legs. Mrs. Lang had a son named Richard, and Cody knew that Richard was a few years older than he was. He must have married a woman nearly half his age.

Caroline had placed Jarod in his own coat, along with a hat and gloves. She handed Cody back his jacket and he put it on and left it unfastened.

"You were married to Richard?"

17

"No, Bobby, his younger brother. Barbara had Bobby late, when she was forty-two. Bobby died in the army earlier this year."

"I wasn't aware that Richard had a brother, but then, I was away from town for quite a while. I'm sorry to hear about your loss."

Caroline raised herself onto her toes and kissed Cody. "Thanks to you I still have my son." She moved away while holding Jarod. Those assembled smiled at the reunited mother and son.

"Cody may have saved that boy's life. He's a hero!"

Those words came from someone at the rear of the crowd, one of the people who had volunteered to look for Jarod. There were nods of agreement among those gathered.

A figure wearing a gray suit beneath a black cashmere overcoat pushed through the crowd. It was the mayor, Jimmy Kyle, and as usual, he was followed by councilwoman Gail Avery.

The mayor was blond, good-looking, and came from money. He and the chief of police had been reelected to new terms the year before. Chief Mendez had won in a landslide while Jimmy Kyle eked out a victory over his opponent. Gail Avery was the mayor's biggest fan. It was assumed that she had a crush on the man. Avery was a plain-looking, pinched-faced woman who didn't wear makeup and preferred demure clothing. If there was anything going on between them, it was kept private.

"Parker! What were you doing with that boy?"

"I found him on my land, Jimmy."

The mayor turned and looked over at the rear of the Lang house. "You're saying that little boy walked all the way over here without anyone seeing him?"

"I'm saying I found him. I assume he walked here."

"There's a fence. He's too small to climb over it."

"I guess he crawled beneath it. That fence is meant to keep cattle and horses in, not to keep toddlers out."

Chief Mendez spoke up. "What's your problem, Jimmy, you don't like happy endings?"

The mayor's eyes went to the gun holstered on Cody's hip. He pointed at it. "I hope you have a permit for that."

Cody looked over at Mendez. "If I claim he's trespassing, will you arrest the mayor?"

The chief smiled. "Well now, he is on your land, and I don't remember hearing you invite him here."

Jimmy Kyle's face reddened. "You can't arrest me for being here. I was investigating the welfare of a citizen, a child."

"The boy is fine, so why don't you leave now?" Cody said.

The mayor was gearing up to respond when a

beefy man in a John Deere cap jostled him to stand before Cody and stick out his hand. The man was named Fergus. Cody and the chief had grown up with him.

As Cody shook his hand, Fergus patted him on the shoulder. "You might have saved that kid's life, Cody."

"All I did was come across him, Fergus. It was luck."

"Luck is right," the mayor said. "It could have been anybody."

Fergus released Cody's hand and spun on Jimmy Kyle. The mayor had also been a classmate of theirs. He and Fergus had been friends at that time. The situation had changed. Jimmy had dated Fergus's younger sister while in college and had broken her heart by cheating on her. That ended the friendship between Jimmy and Fergus.

"Luck, hmm, Jimmy? Even if it was luck, so what? Cody has done more for this town since he returned than you've done for it as mayor. I don't know how you managed to get reelected, but it was a mistake. We should have made Cody the mayor instead."

Someone in the crowd seconded that idea, then a third person agreed. The mayor gave Cody a dirty look, spun on his heels and headed back to his car, a late-model Mercedes. Before following Jimmy,

Councilwoman Avery glared at Cody as if he had personally insulted her.

The crowd drifted away soon after, leaving only Steve Mendez behind.

"What was with that dirty look Jimmy gave me?"

"He never did like you, but now he has a reason. You're Mr. Popular in this town, Cody. Even before today, you and Sara donated money to keep the youth center open and helped out the library and the volunteer fire department. Fergus is right. If you had run for mayor, you might have won."

"I'm as apolitical as they come."

"You're still popular, and that worries a weasel like Jimmy."

"It shouldn't. He was just reelected last year."

"He's probably wondering just how popular you'll be by the time the next election rolls around."

"I'll never run for mayor, so he's got nothing to worry about."

"Maybe not from you, but I might run against him next time. The man is a bonehead and is bad for the town."

"You want to be mayor someday, Steve? I thought you liked being a cop."

"I do, but I've been a cop of one kind or another for most of my life; it might be time to make a change in a few years."

"Change is good. I've made a ton of changes over the last year or so."

"I'm glad you returned to town, pardner. It's been great having you back."

Cody smiled. "I'm enjoying it too. For a long time I wouldn't let myself think about the life I once had here because I thought I could never have it again. But being back on the ranch, being myself again... it just feels right."

Mendez leaned in and spoke in a low voice. "You're still acting as Tanner?"

"I'll always be a Tanner, even after I find someone to take my place."

"I guess we both have secrets, and you know mine too."

Mendez was a vigilante. There was a group of law enforcement personnel who referred to themselves as Sword Bearers.

The statue of Lady Justice that could be found outside many courthouses displayed her as carrying scales in her left hand, in which she weighed evidence. In her right hand was a sword, and the sword was a symbol of punishment. Sword Bearers believed it was their duty to mete out that punishment, which usually resulted in the death of the guilty.

As far as Cody was concerned the Sword Bearers were a good thing. The guilty were often allowed to escape punishment in what passed for a system of justice in modern times, and as Tanner, Cody had often exacted vengeance for victims of crimes.

Mendez had told Cody he became involved in law enforcement because of what had happened to Cody and his family decades earlier. That horrific event led to Cody becoming an assassin, while Mendez became a DEA agent, and later, chief of police.

Cody stared at his old friend. "There's something I've been curious about for a while."

"What's that?"

"The Harvey brothers, Rich and Ernie, did you kill them?"

Mendez shook his head. "That wasn't me. Those two bozos were low-level drug dealers, yeah, but they never handled the hard stuff, like meth. I'm not fool enough to try to keep people from smoking weed, but I will give hell to anyone dealing a poison like meth."

"Someone killed the Harvey brothers. Could it have been other drug dealers?"

"Yeah, there's someone out there selling meth and heroin. So far, we've kept it out of Stark. Over in Culver things are different. They've had a couple of kids overdose on heroin this year."

"If you need help eliminating the problem, let me know."

"Is that you saying that, or Tanner?"

"Me. I'm raising a son in this town the same as you are, Steve. I don't want him growing up in a cesspool."

"Maybe I'll take you up on that offer when I find out who's behind the drugs. I don't plan to arrest them so that they can just get released by a soft-hearted judge."

"Death is what they deserve. If you don't kill them, I will."

"Now that sounded like Tanner."

Cody smiled. "It did, didn't it?"

2

FEARLESS

WESTERN PENNSYLVANIA

THE YOUTH MOTOCROSS EVENT WAS WINDING DOWN as the top two racers battled for the lead well ahead of the rest of the pack. One of them was fifteen-year-old Henry Knight.

Henry was behind a boy named Tony Gray who kept weaving his bike back and forth across the track to deny Henry an opportunity to speed by him. With only one lap to go, it looked like Henry would come in at second place.

The racers sped over the hills and dips of the track with Henry breathing down Gray's neck while looking for an opening he could use to rocket past the other boy. It was no use. Gray was keeping him blocked.

Seated in the stands was Henry's grandmother, Laura, and his girlfriend, Makayla. Makayla was a year older than Henry and was a stunningly beautiful girl with auburn curls and huge blue eyes. She had grown up in Milan, Italy, but spoke English well, and with an accent that only made her more appealing. Her family had moved to the Pittsburgh region after her father had been promoted and transferred to the United States. Makayla and Henry had been dating for three months and were inseparable.

Laura had her hands clutched together in her lap. She was an attractive woman in her late forties. She had given birth to Henry's mother when she was Makayla's age and Henry's late mother had followed suit, having Henry when she was only sixteen.

"That Tony Gray won't give Henry a chance to get past him," Laura said.

Makayla grinned. "That won't stop Henry."

She was right. With less than half a lap to go, Henry hugged the right-side edge of the track. Just when it looked as if Henry might run into the rear of Gray's bike, Gray's dirt bike headed down a slope. As for Henry, he went airborne. Henry squeezed every ounce of power he could get out of the 250cc engine and leapt over not one, or two, but three hills. He landed beside Gray who had navigated the rises one by one. Henry then took the lead as he sped away from an astonished Gray. Thirty seconds later, Henry was declared the winner of the race.

MAKAYLA SAT BESIDE HENRY IN THE FRONT SEAT OF Laura's pickup truck and held the trophy Henry had won. After kissing Henry, she asked a question.

"How many trophies is this, six?"

"Yeah, and my sponsor said he's going to get me a new bike too." Henry leaned forward to look past Makayla and at Laura. "The old bike is mine to do with as I please, Grandma. I'll sell it and give you the money. That should help out, hmm?"

"It will help," Laura said. "But I'll only take some of it. You've got college to save for."

"I know. I'm just glad I can help with the bills. And I know it costs money to travel to these events."

Laura laughed. "Not when you're as successful as you've been, they don't. There's no prize money, but your sponsor covers our expenses. They know a winner when they see one, Henry. If you decide to go pro when you're older, they want to be right there."

"I can't wait until I'm sixteen. Then I can move up to the bikes with more power."

"And I'll have more gray hairs. That leap you made looked dangerous."

"I've leapt higher during practice," Henry said, as he ran a hand through his dark hair.

THEY STOPPED AT A RESTAURANT ON THE HIGHWAY FOR dinner before heading home to the town they lived in near Pittsburgh. As they left the truck to head inside the eatery, no one noticed the two men parking an old white van nearby. The van had been following them all day.

The men were named Vernon and Sal. They were both twenty-eight and had been criminals since they were younger than Henry. They currently made their living by abducting teen girls. Makayla was their target. They were just waiting for the right time to grab her.

Sal pointed at Makayla. He had brown hair while Vernon's was a shade of dirty blond.

"Look at the ass on that girl. We'll get top dollar for her."

"Oh yeah we will. It's why we paid Griffey extra when he showed us the pictures he took of her. She's even hotter in person."

"I'm tired of following them around though. We

need to get to her without the woman and the boy around."

Vernon tossed a thumb toward the back of the van. "That's where she comes in."

Sitting on the floor of the rear of the van was an eight-year-old girl named Ellie. She would be the bait used to hook Makayla.

LAURA AND MAKAYLA WENT TO THE LADIES' ROOM together, but Makayla finished first and told Laura that she would see her back at the table. As Makayla stepped out of the ladies' room and into a hallway, she spotted Ellie, who appeared to be crying. Ellie had strawberry locks that were as long and curly as Makayla's but appeared tangled and uncombed. Her sunken eyes were a deep green. Ellie was small for her age and too skinny.

Makayla went to her. "What's the matter, honey?"

"My daddy is sick. He's out there," Ellie said, as she pointed in the direction of the parking lot.

Makayla looked startled and took the girl by the hand. "Take me to your father." She began pulling Ellie toward the front of the restaurant then felt resistance.

"No. Daddy parked back here," Ellie said.

There was a rear door at the end of the hallway

that led to the back of the restaurant. Ellie began guiding Makayla toward it and Makayla followed. As she did so, she took out her phone to call Henry.

HENRY ANSWERED HIS PHONE AND HEARD MAKAYLA'S voice. She sounded worried.

"I'm at the rear of the restaurant with a little girl. She said her papa was sick. I'm going to see how bad he—" Makayla's next words were muffled, that was followed by the sound of her phone hitting the ground.

"Makayla? Hey, are you all right?"

There was no answer, although Henry could hear sounds through the phone. He rose from the table and headed outside. Makayla had said that she was at the rear of the building. Henry ran around the restaurant and arrived in time to see two men shoving Makayla into the open side door of a van. Makayla wasn't struggling and looked as if she'd been drugged, as her head lolled from side to side. The little girl Makayla had mentioned was inside the van as well. As Makayla was settled into it, the girl began attaching plastic ties to her wrists.

"Hey! Stop. Help! Somebody help!"

There was no one else around and no windows faced the rear of the restaurant. Henry rushed toward the van as the side door was slammed shut. He reached the vehicle just as it began moving but couldn't grasp the door handle. Sal's face was reflected in the side-view mirror. He was laughing at Henry.

As the van gained speed to head around the other side of the building, Henry turned to rush toward his grandmother's truck. He came to a skidding halt when he saw Makayla's phone lying on the ground. After scooping it up, he shoved it into the front pocket of his denim jacket.

Henry rounded the building in time to see the van head onto the highway. He lowered the truck's liftgate and climbed into the rear, where he began undoing the straps holding his dirt bike in place. The van was still in sight as the traffic on the highway was heavy but moving at a steady pace.

Henry shoved his helmet on his head and revved up his bike to send it spurting out of the back of the truck. His phone was vibrating inside his pocket. Although he knew it must be his grandmother wondering what had happened to him and Makayla, Henry ignored it. All his concentration was devoted to catching up to the van.

The traffic was flowing along at around sixty. That was good, because Henry's bike could barely reach a top speed of seventy. He pushed the bike to its limit as he closed in on the van. When the vehicle began weaving its way among the traffic, Henry realized he'd been spotted.

Sᴀʟ ᴡᴀs ɪɴ ᴛʜᴇ ᴘᴀssᴇɴɢᴇʀ sᴇᴀᴛ ᴀɴᴅ ᴡᴀᴛᴄʜɪɴɢ Henry in the mirror. "That little shit is catching up. If a cop sees him chasing us, we might get pulled over too."

Vernon pointed ahead. "There's a side road about a mile away that leads to an old gravel yard. I'll turn in there and we can deal with that prick."

Mᴀᴋᴀʏʟᴀ's ᴘʜᴏɴᴇ ʀᴀɴɢ ɪɴ Hᴇɴʀʏ's ᴘᴏᴄᴋᴇᴛ. Iᴛ ᴡᴀs Laura. Since she couldn't contact Henry, she was trying Makayla's phone. Now that he felt confident of keeping the van in sight, Henry took out the phone to talk to her.

Between the helmet and the wind whipping by he couldn't make out his grandmother's words. He hoped that she could hear him.

"Grandma! Two guys in a van took Makayla. We're headed west on the highway." Henry proceeded to give his grandmother the license plate number of the van. Her reply was lost to the wind, and when the van slowed and made a right onto a gravel road, Henry told his grandmother about it then tucked the phone back in his jacket pocket.

The chunks of gravel were larger than normal. They had been designed to knock mud off truck tires leaving the gravel pit. Henry needed both hands to control the bike and had to drop his speed dramatically. Looking ahead, Henry saw how the road dipped and curved. It gave him an idea.

He went off the road and up a slight hill where a flat field lay. Henry got the bike up to a good speed again and ran parallel to the gravel road in a straight line. The lane continued to wind, and he was soon even with the van and looking down at them. When Vernon headed into the next curve, Henry pointed his bike toward them and leapt off the hill.

The back wheel of his bike came down hard on the van and cracked the windshield. Vernon was shaken by the impact and failed to maneuver into the next turn. The old van ran into the side of the hill on the left while going over thirty miles an hour. Vernon cursed as in the back of the van Ellie let out a scream.

AFTER CRASHING ONTO THE VAN HENRY SKIDDED OFF the vehicle's hood and landed on the rough gravel surface of the road. The collision with the windshield had damaged the rear shock absorber on the bike and the vehicle became wobbly. Once Vernon collided into the side of the hill, Henry abandoned the bike and went running toward the van. It never concerned him that he was a fifteen-year-old boy going up against two ruthless men who were likely armed. His sole thought was to rescue Makayla.

SAL HAD STRUCK HIS HEAD AGAINST THE SIDE WINDOW when the crash occurred. As a result of the pain he was feeling, he had clenched his eyes shut. When he opened them and saw Henry rushing toward them, Sal plucked out the gun they kept in the glove box.

He opened his door and stuck the gun out. "Stop, kid, or I'll blow your fucking head off."

Henry kept coming, moving as fast as he could, fearless.

Sal aimed the gun at Henry's determined young face and pulled the trigger.

3

MAKE THE CALL

STARK, TEXAS

A⏤т about the time H⏤enry had been winning his race, Cody had been riding along slowly on his horse while holding his infant son. Lucas was all smiles, as he loved being in the saddle.

"He's a born rancher," Cody told Sara. Sara was riding beside Cody on her mare, Misty. She grinned as she looked over at Lucas.

"I can't wait until he's old enough to ride along on his own horse."

"It will happen, and someday I'll teach him to rope cattle. That is, as soon as we get some. If the weather conditions stay good, I say we buy a hundred head of cattle to start, along with a few bulls for breeding."

"Then it will be a real ranch again, like when you were a boy."

They came to the other home on their property. It had once belonged to a family named Kinney. Cody and Sara had lived there for months as their new home was built. The house had been sitting vacant for weeks.

"We need to decide what to do with this house, Cody. It's such a waste to let it go unused."

"I could convert it into living quarters for the training academy I plan to build, but it's some distance from that section of the ranch."

"Maybe we could offer it to Romeo and Nadya. It would be great to have them living here."

"I'd like that too, but they've decided to move to Corpus Christi."

"We'll put it off for now. When spring comes, we'll decide what to do."

"Yeah, there's no rush."

"Let's head back. I don't want to keep Lucas out in the cold for too long. I also have to make dinner."

"What are you making?"

"Roast chicken. I prepared it before we left and just need to place it in the oven."

"Sounds good, and this weather gives me an appetite."

"Oh, Daddy called while you were out earlier. He wants us to come for a visit soon. He said he misses his grandson."

"We'll make plans when Doc gets back. Since we'll be in Connecticut, I'll drive into New York and visit Joe."

"How are things in New York City?"

"Joe said he was busy getting the Giacconi Family back to full strength. They lost a lot of people during their war with Gant."

"Has there been any new trouble?"

"No, but there's always someone out there looking to take over."

By the time they made it back home, Lucas was asleep. Cody settled his son into his crib then took Sara by the hand.

"Lucas has the right idea. I think we should go to bed too."

Sara smiled. "Are you sleepy?"

Cody brushed back her hair. "Not in the least."

"I thought you were hungry?"

"I have all sorts of appetites."

"I've noticed, and you're insatiable too."

"I am when it comes to you."

Sara pulled him along by the hand. "Let's get you to bed. You're not the only one with a craving."

They left their son's nursery and disappeared into their bedroom.

~

AN INSTANT BEFORE SAL'S GUN WENT OFF, HENRY leapt at the open door of the van. His feet slammed against the door with the full force of his bodyweight as a bullet passed over his shoulder.

Sal released a scream of pain as the edge of the door smashed his forearm against the metal frame, breaking a bone. The gun slipped from his hand and bounced beneath the vehicle.

Vernon tried to open his door to get out, but it was wedged against the hill he had collided with. He moved past Sal, who was cradling his broken arm, and stumbled out to confront Henry.

Henry had made it to his feet. He charged at Vernon and hit him with a right. Although only fifteen, Henry's punch had enough force to cause pain and make Vernon's nose bleed. It also enraged Vernon. Vernon was not fifteen, was a full-grown man, and had spent years inside a prison with little else to do but lift weights. He landed a punch on Henry's chin that sent the boy staggering backwards. Henry landed on his back and fought to stay conscious. He might have done so, but then Vernon walked over and kicked him on the chin. The blow rendered Henry unconscious.

VERNON WAS RAISING HIS FOOT TO BRING IT DOWN ON Henry's face when Sal called out to him.

"Don't kill the little shit."

"Why not? You almost blew him away."

"I know, but I'm glad I missed. We don't need a murder rap on our asses, and especially not on a kid."

Vernon calmed down. "Shit. You're right. But the prick saw our faces. If we don't do something, he'll be giving our descriptions to the cops."

"Throw him in the back of the van with the girl."

"Give me a syringe so I can make sure he stays out."

"We don't have any more of the drug. We used the last of it on the girl."

"All right, but I'll tie him up and place a hood on him. Damn that kid! Look what he did to the windshield, and he busted my nose."

"He broke my damn arm, but we'd better get out of here before the cops show up. I'll switch the plates while you deal with him."

"Where's the gun?"

"I think it fell under the van."

Vernon reached down and grabbed the phone that was in the front pocket of Henry's jacket. It was Makayla's phone. Henry's cell phone was still in his pants pocket.

Vernon dragged Henry over to the side of the van, then hefted him inside. Henry lay beside Makayla, she was awake but just barely, after having been drugged. A soft moan escaped her as she saw Henry lying beside her.

Without being asked to do so, young Ellie handed Vernon a zip tie from a toolbox that was on the van's floor. Vernon took it and was about to secure Henry's wrists when he was punched in the throat. Henry had begun stirring awake while being dragged along the ground and had feigned unconsciousness until he saw an opening.

Vernon gagged from the punch and was having trouble breathing. Henry hit him again as Vernon fell onto him, delivering an elbow to the side of Vernon's head.

"What the hell is going on in there?" Sal cried out. He was outside the van on his knees trying to reach the gun he had dropped.

Henry slid the side door open and leapt on Sal. Sal released a cry of shock followed by a howl of pain as he tumbled backwards to land on his broken arm. Henry began pummeling the man with punches to the face. Sal, with one good arm, struggled to block the blows.

ZAP!

Henry grunted as 50,000 volts coursed through his body. He'd been zapped with a stun gun. The weapon belonged to Vernon, who had used it earlier when he came up behind Makayla. It wasn't Vernon using it now, it was Ellie. The little girl had freed the weapon off Vernon's belt and used it to stun Henry.

Sal sat up, his face bloody and his lip split open from Henry's blows. After snatching the stun gun from Ellie, Sal gave Henry a second taste of the weapon.

Afterward, Henry was secured with zip ties. As an added measure, Sal covered Henry's head with a shopping bag so he couldn't see, then used a knife to cut an air hole in the top of it. With only one arm, it had taken some effort for Sal to load Henry into the van. Once that was done, he checked on Vernon.

Henry's blow had done damage to Vernon's throat. He was sitting up in the rear of the van and breathing raggedly while releasing a hideous gasping sound.

"Shit, Vernon. I should have let you kill the bastard."

Vernon managed to squeeze out a few hoarse words. "Get us... out of here."

As Sal was turning to climb into the front of the

van, Vernon grabbed the sleeve of his good arm. "Make... the call... we need help."

Sal winced at the suggestion. "You sure about that? Lennox is not going to be happy that we fucked things up."

Vernon nodded. "Just...make...the call."

"All right, but first I'll get us back to base."

Ellie spoke up. "I helped. I did good."

"Yeah, kid," Sal said. "You did really good."

"So, can I eat?"

Sal unlocked a blue plastic cooler that was secured to the driver's side of the van's wall. There were wrapped bologna sandwiches inside sitting atop ice, along with several juice boxes. He tossed Ellie one of the sandwiches and a drink. The little girl tore apart the wrapper and began eating ravenously. It was her first meal in two days. Sal grabbed another bologna sandwich and handed it to Ellie.

"You get a second one for helping with the boy."

Ellie smiled up at him as if he had just given her the gift she'd wanted most for Christmas.

Sal locked up the cooler, then assisted Vernon and settled him up front in the passenger seat. Every step Vernon took made it more difficult for him to breathe. Sal wondered if Henry had come close to crushing Vernon's windpipe

The van was in running condition. Being an

older vehicle, no airbags had deployed when it crashed. Along with its cracked windshield was a dented side panel from the collision with the hill. Sal decided to stay off the highway and used a navigation app on his phone to find a series of back roads that would take them to their destination.

In the rear of the van, Henry groped around with his bound hands until he found Makayla. He took one of her limp hands and gave it a squeeze. She responded by mumbling his name before the drug dragged her under again. He had failed her, and now they were both in trouble. Despite that, Henry vowed that he would somehow save her.

The van bumped along the uneven gravel road and toward a dark future.

4

SEEN TOO MUCH

PENNSYLVANIA

SAL HAD CALLED AND LEFT A MESSAGE FOR THE MAN IN charge of their operation and he had sent his representative to handle things, a man named Armstrong.

They were at an old house that had been abandoned a decade earlier. It had a garage and that was where Sal and Vernon were holding the girls they had abducted. There were two other girls besides Makayla. They had both been taken while on dates with a boyfriend. They were kept drugged most of the time and locked inside of metal dog crates, the type used for large hounds.

Armstrong was a black man in his thirties with a

shaved head. He arrived with three other men and a woman inside a motor home. The woman and one of the men were in their seventies and looked like a pair of retirees. They were always up in the front of the RV in case a cop looked in while passing by. The old man even wore a fishing hat and smoked a pipe. He looked like the typical retired grandfather.

Sal knew the man had spent decades as a pimp and later became a white slaver when he realized it was less work and more profit. The old woman playing his wife had been one of his earliest hookers and later became the madam of a whore house. Everyone called them Gramps and Granny.

The other two men were muscle and looked the part. They were both huge, ripped, and must have spent hours every day lifting weights. The two seldom spoke and neither had ever said a word to Sal. That was all right with him. The two musclemen looked like nothing but trouble.

Sal didn't know Armstrong's story. He did know that the man gave off a dangerous vibe and that he was Mr. Lennox's trouble shooter. Sal just hoped that he wasn't considered trouble by Armstrong. If so, he might wind up getting shot.

He calmed himself. Things weren't so bad. They managed to get the girl and had avoided the cops. Of course, there was the boy, that damn kid. He had to be dealt with. Knowing Armstrong's reputation, Sal figured he would kill the boy or have him sold off like the girl would be. There wasn't the market for teen boys that there was for girls, but it did exist. The motocross racer was a good-looking kid. He'd probably fetch a fine fee on the market.

Armstrong had sat staring at Sal and Vernon impassively as they told their story. Vernon's breathing had improved some, but he was still wheezing and in a lot of pain. Sal's busted lip had swollen, and it was difficult for him to talk. He had to speak slowly so he didn't lisp. They were inside the dilapidated house with a pair of electric lanterns providing light.

Makayla was in a cage in the garage with the other girls, but Henry had been propped up in a corner of one of the rooms upstairs. The shopping bag still covered his head and he was still bound by plastic ties.

When Sal finished his story, Armstrong began asking questions.

"How old is the boy?"

Sal shrugged. "Maybe fifteen, sixteen."

"Did he have a weapon?"

"No."

"But you had a pistol and a stun gun, and there were two of you."

"Yeah, but Mr. Armstrong, the kid got lucky."

"If he were any luckier you two might be in jail,

or he might have killed your asses. You both look like shit. And why are you holding your arm like that, is it broken?"

Sal nodded. "It got caught in the van door when the kid kicked it."

"And he saw your faces?"

"Well, yeah."

Armstrong was quiet as he continued to stare at Sal and Vernon.

Sal cleared his throat. "We could sell the boy too, you know? There are guys out there that would want him. That way he wouldn't be a problem and we could all make a little more money. And did you see the girl?"

"I saw her."

"That's some primo ass. I bet Mr. Lennox gets top dollar for her."

"He will. Did the boy have a phone on him?"

"We ditched it at the scene where he caught up to us. I crushed it with a rock."

"You did at least one thing right. What about the girl's phone?"

"That got tossed away where we grabbed her."

Armstrong stood. "Take me to the boy."

"He's upstairs with a bag clamped over his head so he can't see."

"He's already seen too much."

~

HENRY HEARD THE MEN COMING UP THE STAIRS. IT sounded like at least three sets of footsteps. He was locked inside a room that had two mattresses on the floor. He had tripped over both of them as he had explored blindly with the shopping bag still on his head. It was attached by a plastic tie fastened to his neck; the tie was cutting into his flesh.

He had managed to get up each time he'd fallen and moved about by shuffling his bound feet. In an attempt to get free, he was rubbing the plastic restraints against what felt like the edge of a closet doorway. It was having little effect on the cuffs.

The door opened and the men walked in. One of them was Vernon. As Henry heard the rasping sound he was making, he smiled beneath the bag.

"I should have hit you in the throat a little harder; if I had you'd be dead."

Vernon's already red face blushed darker at Henry's words. He rushed forward and landed a punch at the center of the shopping bag.

A grunt came from beneath the bag as Henry's knees buckled. He succeeded in keeping his feet under him and leaned back against the doorframe of the closet.

"Take off these cuffs and fight me. I bet I kick your ass."

Vernon was wheezing in greater volume after his exertion, but he reared back a fist to strike Henry again.

"Leave the boy alone," Armstrong said. Henry heard the voice and was certain it hadn't belonged to either of the two men he had fought.

Sal grabbed Vernon's sleeve and pulled him back. "Yeah, man. We don't want to mess up his face. If he stays pretty, we'll get more for him when we sell him."

Armstrong took out his gun. "We're not selling him. He's seen too much."

Henry stiffened. He'd heard the sound of a slide being pulled back as Armstrong chambered a round. When Armstrong fired the gun, Henry jumped at the sound. Armstrong had shot off four rounds in quick succession, the blasts' reverberation was still echoing throughout the room when the thud of Vernon and Sal's bodies hitting the floor reached Henry's ears.

Armstrong gathered the spent shell casings, the men's wallets, and their phones. He was heading out of the room when Henry called to him.

"Where's Makayla? Is she all right?"

"Forget about her. You're never going to see her again. There are a lot of girls out there. Just grab yourself another one."

Armstrong left the room as Henry threatened

him. "I'll find her, and I'll kill anyone who's harmed her."

Armstrong's derisive laughter pierced Henry, and he slumped to the floor with a feeling of helplessness and despair.

5

A PLEA FOR HELP

PENNSYLVANIA

THE FBI ARRIVED ON THE SCENE WITH THE STATE police an hour after Armstrong and the others had cleared out with the girls. They had located the property thanks to Henry. While in the van he had slipped his phone out of his pocket and left it wedged behind something made of metal. He had still been unable to see but thought the object felt like a toolbox.

The van had been left at the scene and had been torched with gasoline. The fire hadn't destroyed the cell phone before the authorities were able to triangulate its position. The old abandoned home was the fourth structure in the area that the state police and the Feds had checked out.

When the shopping bag was removed from Henry's head, he enjoyed the feeling of fresh air on his sweaty face. Afterward, Henry saw the bodies of Sal and Vernon. Armstrong had shot them each in the head and heart.

"Where's Makayla?"

An FBI special agent named Kyle Croft assured Henry that they were still searching for her while freeing his wrists and ankles from the plastic restraints binding them. Agent Croft was in his early thirties but had years of experience working abduction cases.

Makayla and the other two caged girls had been loaded onto the RV and driven away. Thanks to the fire in the van evidence of the other abductions was destroyed. Henry was unaware that the other girls had been there. He would be unable to provide any help in that area.

Agent Croft was interested in hearing everything Henry could tell him about Ellie. A child had been involved in a number of recent abductions throughout western Pennsylvania and eastern Ohio. From Henry's description of her it sounded like Ellie might be the young girl they had been looking for.

"Why the hell would she help those scumbags?" Henry asked.

"Maybe she doesn't know any better," Agent Croft said.

"You mean she's the daughter of one of the men who took Makayla, and that they trained her to help them?"

"That's possible. It's more likely that she was abducted as well, at a very young age."

Henry looked disgusted. "They snatched a kid then taught her to trick girls out to the van?"

"It looks that way. I'll send someone back to that restaurant to see what they might have on their security cameras. Right now, I want to get you to a hospital and have you checked out. They roughed you up a bit. Your grandmother will be there waiting for you. She was worried sick about you."

"I'll be all right. Just find Makayla, please?"

"We'll do our best, Henry."

LAURA ENVELOPED HENRY IN A HUG THEN MOANED AS she took in his battered face.

"Oh, thank God they found you. I was so worried."

"I'm all right, Grandma, but Makayla is still missing."

"I know, honey, but the police and the FBI are doing everything they can to find her."

"They have to find her," Henry said. "They have to."

VIDEO OF ELLIE AND MAKAYLA TALKING IN THE hallway outside the restrooms was obtained from the cameras at the restaurant. Because of the way her hair was hanging down in front of her face, it was difficult to make out Ellie's features.

The outdoor cameras didn't record the abduction. Vernon had positioned the van in a blind spot between cameras. There was video of Henry running around to the rear of the building and of the van racing away. That did the authorities little good. They already had the van and the bodies of Sal and Vernon. All they could do was question the men's relatives and known associates.

IT WAS DECIDED TO HOLD A PRESS CONFERENCE OUT IN front of the police station the following morning to seek the public's help. Makayla's grandfather was a magistrate in Italy who had some international clout. There was more pressure than usual to find the missing girl. Makayla's parents asked that they be given a chance to speak. They wanted to plead with Makayla's abductors to return their child safely.

Henry attended the press conference with his grandmother. His face displayed signs of the abuse he'd suffered. He had wanted to speak as well but was told that he couldn't. He was a minor and Agent Croft thought it best that the boy remain out of the spotlight. The truth was, Croft had feared he would find Henry dead the day before. Early in his career he had lost a young child named Maria Ortiz to a kidnapper. That death haunted him still.

Finding Henry alive had been the highlight of Croft's year. If they could somehow save Makayla and others like her who were abducted to be used as sex slaves, Croft would feel as if he had atoned a little for his past sins. He still blamed himself for losing Maria.

Makayla's parents made an impassioned plea for her safe return while asking the public for help. As the press conference was winding down, Henry left his grandmother's side and walked up to the podium.

Agent Croft placed a hand on Henry's shoulder to ease him away. Henry shrugged him off and spoke to the reporters gathered.

"My name is Henry Knight. I'm Makayla's boyfriend and I was there when she was taken. I know the police and the FBI are doing all they can to find her, but I'm hoping someone else will look for her too. Someone helped me a few years ago when I was still a kid. If that man is listening... I'm begging you, please help me again. I... I love Makayla. Please find her. If anyone can do it, I know you can."

The reporters began shouting questions at Henry as others snapped photos of his bruised face.

Agent Croft ended the press conference and guided Henry and Makayla's parents back inside the station.

HOURS LATER, IN THE TEXAS TOWN OF STARK, CODY and Sara were stunned as they watched the press conference. It had been repeated on the six o'clock news. After viewing it, Sara rewound the video, then paused on an image of Henry's face. Cody got up from the sofa and walked over to the TV to stare at the image.

"That's Henry," Sara said. "*Our* Henry. He looks so much older."

"Yes."

"He was talking about you, because of how you saved him and his family from Boyd Kessler."

"Yeah. If I hadn't gotten there when I did, Kessler would have burned them all to death."

"What are you going to do, Cody?"

Cody placed a hand on the television. "I'm going to Pennsylvania and find that girl."

"Do you really think you can?"

"I'll do my best, and I'll go through anyone that gets in my way."

"I'll come with you. I want to see Henry again."

"What about the baby?"

"I'll drop him off with Daddy for a few hours while I visit Henry, then I'll go back to Connecticut and wait for you."

Cody grimaced at the image on the screen, at the emotional pain visible in Henry's eyes.

"That boy is hurting. I know what it's like to have someone you love snatched away from you. At least there's a good chance this Makayla is still alive."

Sara joined him in front of the television and kissed him.

"Agent X to the rescue?"

Cody's intense eyes looked at the TV again. "It will be more like Agent X on the hunt. And when I find the men who have that girl, there won't be anyone left for the police to arrest."

6
GATHERING INFO

NEW YORK CITY

THE AIR WAS COLD AND THE SKY A BRIGHT BLUE AS Tanner entered a quiet coffee shop in the mid-morning hours. He ignored the few patrons and employees and headed down a short corridor. A door opened and a man stepped out to greet him. The man was named Duke.

Duke owned the coffee shop as a cover for a unique business. He could get you practically anything on the black market if you could afford it. He met with select clients in the back room of the shop. Duke had a beefy build, salt-and-pepper hair cropped short, and a nose made crooked by having been broken many times. He and Tanner shook hands after Tanner was escorted inside the back room.

"I was surprised but pleased when I got your call, Tanner. It's been awhile."

"Sara and I are living the quiet life these days. Or I guess I should say, most days."

Duke smiled. "I was able to get everything you asked for."

"Including the Jeep?"

"Yeah, and it's all waiting for you at this address." Duke handed Tanner a slip of paper with a location written on it. The address was in Pittsburgh.

"Thanks for doing a rush job on this, Duke."

"No thanks needed. You paid extra. Speaking of extra, I have something you might like."

"What's that?"

Duke pointed to a table where a cell phone sat. "That's a little something a supplier gave me. If it works like he says, I could see where it could come in handy for a guy like you."

"A phone?"

Duke shook his head. "It's not a phone. Well, it is a real phone, but it's something else too." Duke went on to explain what it was. And Tanner seemed interested.

"I haven't tried one out yet," Duke said. "But I saw

a video and the damn thing is great. You can even activate it by using another phone."

"How much are they?"

"I've got three samples left. Take two as a gift for all the business you give me."

Tanner took a case containing two of the "phones" and thanked Duke.

"I'll call you if I need anything else, although by then I'll be in Pennsylvania."

"Happy hunting."

"Hunting is what it will be."

TANNER'S NEXT STOP WAS THE OFFICE BUILDING JOE Pullo was using as an office. The strip club Johnny R's had been leveled by a bomb set off during the war with the Gant Family. It was a war the Giacconis won at a great price.

Pullo smiled as he shook Tanner's hand and welcomed him inside his office. It was a large space that had two desks, sofas, and a wet bar.

"It's good to have you back in New York, buddy. How are Sara and Lucas?"

"They're both good. What about Laurel and Johnny?"

"Laurel's perfect, and Johnny gets bigger every day."

Tanner pointed at Joe's left leg. Pullo had injured it during the explosion when his knee became hyperextended. The last time Tanner saw him, Joe had to use a cane to get around.

"I see you're healed."

"Yeah, but the leg still aches a little some days. I'm just glad I don't have a limp."

"Maybe you should run a few laps to strengthen it."

"I haven't done any running yet, but I've started working out again. There's a boxing gym I own a piece of, and I've been going there three times a week. Maybe it's because I'm getting older, but I was gaining weight after I hurt my leg and couldn't move around as much as usual. If a guy in my position gets fat it could cost me my life someday."

"A boxing gym is a good place to get in shape."

"Yeah, I talked Finn Kelly into being my sparring partner. He thinks I should start running too. But enough about my leg. What brings you here?"

"This is a brief visit. I have business to see to in Pennsylvania. I was hoping you might be able to help."

"Just tell me what you need, and I'll see what I can do."

"I need information."

Tanner explained that he was looking for a lead on who might have abducted Makayla.

"I saw that on the news last night. That was you the kid was talking about?"

"Yeah. Sara and I met Henry when he was just ten. The kid was on the scene when I made a hit."

"And he's kept his mouth shut. That's a good kid."

"I helped him with a problem then and I want to do the same now, but I need a place to start."

Joe and Tanner had taken seats on a sofa. Joe stood and began pacing as he thought things through.

"Illegal activities are my business, but the Giacconi Family has never been involved in sex trafficking and never will be."

"I know that, Joe. We wouldn't be friends if you were into that sort of thing. But like you said, illegal activities are your business. I was hoping you might know of someone or have an idea about who would be in that trade."

Joe nodded. "I don't know anyone, but I might know someone who would. Sit tight, Tanner. I need to make a few phone calls."

While Joe settled behind his desk, Tanner went to the bar and grabbed a beer from a small refrigerator. As he sipped on the brew, he took out his phone and checked to see if there was any news about Makayla. There was none, but the video showing Henry's impassioned plea for help was getting wide coverage. The media and other commentators were wondering who it was Henry had been addressing, and what was the help the mystery man had given the boy in the past.

Speculation arose about events surrounding the death of Henry's mother. Tanner was surprised to learn that there had been a development in that case. Boyd Kessler, the man who had murdered Henry's mother, Laura, wasn't who he had claimed to be. The body of the real Boyd Kessler had been uncovered in California as a wildfire ravaged a section of woodland.

The real Boyd Kessler had been stabbed multiple times and shoved into a shallow grave. The grave was uncovered as firefighters were digging a fire break. Along with the corpse was an orange jumpsuit. It had belonged to an escaped prisoner named Brock Kessler, Boyd's lookalike older brother.

It was theorized that Brock, who had been serving time for arson and assault, had contacted his brother and asked him for help after he and two other inmates escaped from a county jail. Brock then murdered Boyd to assume his identity. The two men weren't twins, but they had similar builds, were both tall, and bore a strong resemblance to each other. However, Brock had four gold teeth. Authorities believed he was still alive and on the run. He was not. Tanner had killed the man as he was attempting to burn Henry and his family to death.

Brock Kessler was no longer a problem. Finding Makayla alive and killing the men who took her was what mattered now.

Pullo left his desk and walked over to the bar. He was holding a slip of paper with a name and an address on it.

"There's a scumbag named Vince Decker who lives in the Atlantic City area. Decker was once a member of the Philly mob. He got into trouble with his capo for selling underaged girls to a Venezuelan gang. That gang is no longer active, but Decker might still be in the business and know something."

"How good do you think this lead is?"

"Let's call it B+. The guy I spoke with said that Decker had a thing for teenage girls. Before he began selling them, he was getting them hooked on heroin and having them rent themselves out."

"He was a pimp?"

"Yeah, but that was years ago. These days he's probably at the point where he has other guys run the girls for him. They say he's done well since leaving Philadelphia and is in good with the Jersey mob. I hope that helps you, Tanner."

"So do I, and thanks, Joe. Once I get Decker to talk, then I'll move on to the next link in the chain, and after that, the next one."

Pullo laughed. "That means there are a bunch of guys out there that are going to have a very bad day."

"And likely their last," Tanner said.

He downed the rest of his beer, shook Pullo's hand, then headed to New Jersey.

7

THE FIRST LINK IN THE CHAIN

SMITHVILLE, NEW JERSEY

VINCE DECKER LIVED IN A HOUSE THAT SAT ON SEVEN acres and was about fifteen miles west of Atlantic City. It was a quiet street and most of his neighbors were professionals. Decker was also a professional. He was a professional scumbag.

He pimped out his first girl, his cousin, Caroline, when they were both only sixteen. They had run away from home together to escape an abusive male relative who got pleasure by beating them with a belt.

At first, Decker had his cousin use her body so that they could get money to eat. Later on, he used her and two other girls as a way to make money for drugs to sell. By the time he was nineteen he had a stable of six girls and was dealing pot on the side.

To keep the peace and avoid getting killed during a territorial dispute with an older pimp, Decker had given the man his cousin and one other girl. The gift had been temporary and a way to lull the rival into believing he was weak. Days later, Decker snuck into the man's condo and shot him to death while he was in the shower. The man hadn't been alone. Decker's cousin, Caroline, had been inside the shower with him. Decker shot her too, so there would be no witnesses.

He eventually hooked up with the mob in Philadelphia. With their backing, his stable of hookers rose to more than thirty. Decker became rich and life was good, but Decker always sought to have more.

He knew that the mob wanted nothing to do with trafficking girls, despite the immense profit to be had. At the time, the trade was controlled by a Venezuelan street gang that was a target of the FBI. Getting involved with them brought with it too much risk. Besides, why sell a girl once when you could rent her out for years?

Decker didn't see it that way. He had grown tired of being a pimp and the endless need to keep his hookers in line. Turning a runaway into a prostitute took time and energy. Decker had to woo them, be their friend, and act as if he was the only one in the world who gave a damn about them. Once he had earned their trust, he could convince them to do almost anything. Unlike some pimps, he had hated the playacting, flattering, and persuasion it took to develop a hooker. He much preferred slapping them around when they got out of line. Selling women and being done with them sounded pretty good to him.

He started by selling off the youngest girls in his stable. They had all been high moneymakers but also high maintenance. Decker used some of his profits to enlist men to be "recruiters" for him. Their only task was to locate girls between the ages of thirteen and seventeen who were beautiful.

One of the men was exceptional at finding such girls. His secret? He staked out casting calls whenever someone was filming a commercial for teen girls. At one such audition, the man had managed to steal a file that contained the list of candidates, this included photos, along with their names, phone numbers, and home addresses. Seven of those girls went missing in the following days. Not one of them was ever seen again.

It didn't take the cops long to find the link that connected the girls. The youngest was fourteen and the oldest was seventeen. They had all been aspiring models and had auditioned for a commercial that would be selling tanning lotion.

When the heat was turned up on the investigation it led to the FBI arresting the man who had stolen the file. The fool had left his prints behind on the filing cabinet he'd taken the documents from.

He was more than willing to rat out the others involved for a lighter sentence. Fortunately for Decker, there was a team of two men separating him from the snitch. The men who had actually abducted the girls. Decker got to those men only minutes before the cops arrived at the bar the men hung out at. Decker had gone in there wearing a ski mask and carrying a shotgun. He wanted to make it look as if the two had been killed during a robbery. To make it look good, Decker also killed the bartender and seriously wounded two other customers. With the men dead, any link to Decker died with them. Or so he thought.

Eventually, word got back to Decker's capo that he was selling girls to a gang. That same gang was a rival in the drug trade. Decker had his stable of girls taken away and was told to leave Philly. He did so without hesitation, knowing he was lucky his boss hadn't killed him. That had been eighteen years ago.

Nowadays, Decker sat at the top of an operation that ran hookers in Atlantic City for the Jersey mob.

Every now and then, he came across a fresh-faced innocent he could sell to an acquaintance he knew in Pittsburgh. That friend was a part of the gang who took Makayla.

AS WAS HIS HABIT, DECKER, A CONFIRMED NIGHT OWL, had risen around noon, after having been up most of the night. After checking his phone to catch up on news, he made calls to the three men who ran his operation for him. As usual, there had been several petty problems with the girls, and one of the johns had gotten a little rough. They had been handled, and an envelope of cash would be delivered to the house later in the day.

Decker texted his cook who was also his housekeeper and told her what he wanted for lunch, a hot corned beef sandwich on rye with a side of coleslaw, a dill pickle, and a frosty mug of Guinness. She texted back that it would all be ready at the time he requested.

Decker then went to the rear of the home, down a back staircase, and entered the room that held his indoor pool. At forty-eight, Decker was still trim; he attributed it to the swimming he did every day.

After completing his usual fifty laps, Decker climbed from the pool while anticipating his meal.

He was drying his hair when he opened his eyes and saw a pair of feet facing him. The feet were clad in black boots.

He lowered the towel and found himself face-to-face with Tanner. In Tanner's right hand was a gun with a sound suppressor attached.

"Whatever you're being paid to kill me, I can pay more."

"I want information. You can give it to me."

Those words reduced the rapid beating of Decker's heart. If the guy wanted him to rat out someone, that was fine, as long as he got out of it alive.

"What is it you want to know?"

"There's a girl missing in Pennsylvania. Her name is Makayla Albertini. Her photo is all over the news."

Decker nodded and pointed toward his phone. It was sitting atop a nearby table. "I saw that story about her a short time ago, but hey, that wasn't me. I don't know anything about that."

"You know someone who was involved."

"No, man. Honest, I don't know who took that bitch."

Tanner sent a kick into Decker's midsection that caused the pimp to double over.

"You know a name. Someone in that part of Pennsylvania who could be involved. Give me that name."

Decker gasped in pain as he straightened up. "I don't know if he's involved, but there's this dude, yeah, Griffey, he uh, he makes pornos."

"Are you telling me they plan to use Makayla in a sex film?" Tanner asked.

"No. Griffey's into porn, but he's also a recruiter."

"A recruiter?"

"Yeah, he scouts out a certain type of girl. You know, the young hot things, but not just any. They have to be tens, like the one who was taken. That's Griffey's specialty."

"Where can I find him?"

"How the hell would I know? He's somewhere in the Pittsburgh area, or he was. I haven't worked with him in a long time."

"How did you get in touch?"

"Email. I leave a message as a draft and Griffey responds to it."

"You're going to do just that, and you'll set up a meeting too."

"A meeting? Griffey and I don't meet. I've only seen him once, and that was years ago."

"I don't care how you do it, but I need to find out where he is."

Decker shivered. He'd been out of the pool long enough to feel the chill on his wet skin. He usually liked the smell of chlorine, but at that moment it was making him feel queasy.

"Can I have my robe? I'm getting cold."

Tanner brought up the gun and aimed it at Decker's chest. "You're wasting my time."

"Whoa! Calm down. Let me make some calls. Maybe I can get a line on Griffey."

"Do that."

Decker went to the table and picked up his phone. Despite the chill he was feeling, he ignored his robe. He scrolled through his address book then exclaimed when he found a number.

"There's this guy in Pittsburgh, a bookie. Griffey once wrote that he used him a lot. Griffey loved to bet on the races. Maybe he knows where to find Griffey."

"Make the call."

Decker did as ordered. The bookie hadn't spoken with Griffey in over a year, but he heard that he was spending time at a casino in Pittsburgh that sat on the river.

"That's a start. Make more calls."

"Can I have my robe? I'm freezing."

Tanner grabbed the robe, checked the pockets, and when he found nothing, he tossed it to Decker.

"Make those calls."

Twenty minutes later it was confirmed that Griffey spent most evenings at the casino. Not only was he a gambler, but he was also dating one of the bartenders who worked in a restaurant there. Tanner got a description of Griffey from Decker.

"Like I said, I haven't seen him in years, but he's about six two, six three, and built, but not huge like a weightlifter, more like a gymnast."

"What color is his hair?"

"Dark, and he had a beard the one time I'd seen him, a, a goatee. Hey listen, don't let him know that you got his name from me, okay?"

"It won't matter."

"Oh shit, are you going to kill him?"

"Too," Tanner said.

"What?"

"I'm going to kill him too." As he spoke, Tanner angled the gun and fired a round into the center of Decker's forehead.

Thirty minutes later, with his corned beef growing cold and his stout getting flat, Decker's housekeeper went looking for him. When she found his body lying in blood by the pool, she lost her appetite as well.

8

THE RETURN OF AGENT X

HENRY AND HIS GRANDMOTHER WERE IN A SMALL town outside Pittsburgh. Tanner met Sara at the Pittsburgh International Airport, then drove to the area where Henry lived. Sara had taken a flight from Connecticut after dropping Lucas off with his grandfather and her sister, Jenny.

On their previous visit to the area, Henry had given Tanner and Sara directions that were a shortcut to his house, which was at the edge of the town. The path ran along a narrow dirt road that wasn't much wider than a car and was in reality a dry riverbed. It ended in a strip of gravel that met up with the driveway that led to Henry's home.

Tanner and Sara left his SUV along the path and traveled in on foot. The vehicle was the Jeep Tanner had gotten through Duke. It was equipped with hidden compartments for weapons and other supplies. If he needed to, Tanner could abandon the vehicle and not be concerned about it being traced to anyone connected to him. If stopped for a traffic violation, the paperwork would pass inspection.

"I thought there might be a police officer keeping watch," Sara said.

"In a small town like this they probably can't spare anyone for full-time duty. They'll likely drive by once in a while to check on things, or maybe they don't even bother to do more than call."

"I don't like that. Henry could have been killed yesterday. He should be looked after."

"That's why I'm here. I'm going to eliminate the threat."

Although the home's small lawn was cut short and the windows appeared clean, the passing years had not been kind to the house. Paint was peeling in places and the roof appeared to need work. There was also a For Sale sign in the yard.

When he was ten, Henry had been living with his grandmother Laura and her new husband, Glenn. Glenn had two young daughters from a previous marriage. There had been no mention of Glenn or his daughters in the news and Laura was going by the surname of Knight, and not Glenn's name of Olsen. Tanner and Sara figured that meant the two were no longer together.

As for Henry's father, the man was a mystery. Henry had no memory of him, and it seemed his father had left Henry's mother to fend for herself. The only thing Laura ever told Henry about him was that his father was the "biker type."

Tanner rang the bell and heard the sound of chimes come from within. A few moments later, Laura Knight answered the door.

She had seen Tanner twice and Sara only once. That was five years earlier. However, Tanner's eyes were rare. They tended to be remembered.

"Bob?"

That was the name Tanner had been going by at the time. He smiled at Laura.

"Yes, it's us. You remember Sara, don't you?"

A voice spoke up from behind Laura. It wasn't the voice of a man, but neither was it the voice of the boy Tanner remembered.

"Let them in, Grandma."

Laura stepped back and gestured for them to enter. Standing in the living room was Henry. He was smiling in what looked like a mixture of relief and joy at seeing them. In Henry's hands was an old M1 Garand. Tanner had owned one when he was a boy and had fond memories of it.

He had taught Henry how to shoot and care for the weapon the last time he saw him. Back then, the rifle appeared huge in Henry's hands. It now looked like an extension of him.

"Hello, Henry. I got your message."

Henry leaned the rifle against a corner and went to Tanner. After shaking his hand, he gave it a squeeze.

"Thank you. Will you help find Makayla?"

"That's why I'm here, and I've already started."

Henry released Tanner's hand and turned to face Sara. She opened her arms and Henry hugged her.

"Oh, it's so good to see you again, Henry. I've thought about you over the years."

"What's going on here?" Laura asked, as she closed the door.

Tanner pointed toward the kitchen. "Let's talk over coffee."

"Cody Parker?"

"Yes, that's my real name," Tanner told Laura.

He and Sara decided to tell Laura and Henry the truth, or at least, much of it. Tanner went on to tell them about what had happened to him when he was about Henry's age. Members of a Mexican cartel had traveled to the Parker ranch and killed his family. From that point on, he gave them the story he had related when he came back to Stark to reclaim his true identity.

He had been in the WITSEC program, which was commonly known as the Witness Protection. Program. He had stayed in it for decades but after learning that the man who had led the attack on his family was dead, he decided to leave the program and return to Stark, Texas.

Laura was shocked and saddened by the story, as was Henry. But while it appeared Laura believed every word, Tanner detected skepticism in Henry's gaze.

"It must have been frightening to let everyone know that you were alive," Laura said. "Weren't you afraid that someone in the cartel might attack you again?"

"We were attacked," Sara said, "and Cody destroyed them. The Parkers will never leave that land again."

Laura looked down at the ring on Sara's left hand. "You two are married now?"

"Yes, and we have a son."

"Do you have pictures?"

Sara grinned. "Of course I do, and video."

Tanner stood up and Henry did the same. "Henry and I are going to go for a walk. We'll be back in a few minutes."

"Put on a jacket, honey," Laura told Henry. "It's chilly out there."

"Yes, Grandma."

As they were passing through the living room, Henry grabbed his rifle. It had a strap attached and Henry slung the weapon across his back.

They walked down the gravel driveway at a stroll as Henry told Tanner what had happened when Makayla was taken. Tanner listened intently and only asked a few questions, one of those concerned the child who had been helping Vernon and Sal.

"How old do you think she was?"

"Maybe six or seven. Her clothes were dirty, and her hair looked like it hadn't been combed."

"Did she call either of the men her father?"

"No. After she helped, they fed her. I don't think she had eaten in a while. I had my face covered and couldn't see her, but I could hear her chewing. She made fast work of the sandwiches they gave her."

Henry finished his story and they walked back up the driveway. Tanner pointed at the For Sale sign. "Where will you live once the house sells?"

"Grandma said we'll rent an apartment for a few years, until I decide where I'm going to college. Then, maybe she'll buy a smaller house wherever I go to school."

Henry looked sideways at Tanner. "What really happened after your family was killed?"

"I told you. I went into the Witness Protection Program."

Henry was shaking his head. "No. Not you. You wouldn't run and hide. And I'm not a kid anymore, Cody, or should I call you Tanner?"

"You used to call me Agent X."

"You're not an agent, and you didn't go into hiding because you were scared. You don't get scared, do you?"

"Everyone is afraid sometimes."

"Yeah, but you don't let it control you. I've been scared. Right now, I'm so scared for Makayla that it hurts, but if I knew where she was, I would go there to save her even if I had to face an army. You're like that too, only you've really faced off against an army, an army of Mexican drug dealers."

"What do you mean by that?"

"I went online years ago trying to find you. I wanted to stay in contact. All I knew... or all I thought I knew, is that you were an agent, one whose first name was Bob. Sara also called you Tanner, so I went looking for an Agent Bob Tanner. I didn't find one, but there was a lot of talk on the internet back then about an assassin named Tanner. You didn't run and hide from a Mexican cartel; you went down to Mexico and took out the man who killed your family. You killed Alonso Alvarado."

Tanner took in a deep breath then released it

slowly. "You were a bright kid and you're an even smarter teen. Have you ever told anyone about me?"

"No. I've never said a word about what happened to Kessler or mentioned what you did for me. Now that you're here after I've asked for help, Grandma will wonder why."

"I know, but I want to do what I can for you."

"You're really Tanner... the hit man?"

"I like to call myself a trained assassin, but yeah, I'm that Tanner."

Henry blinked rapidly. "You're a legend, but they say you've been around for a hundred years."

"There was a Tanner One; I'm Tanner Seven, and I was trained by my mentor, Tanner Six."

Henry's eyes widened. "Wow. It's like something from the comics."

"Maybe, but I don't wear a cape and I can't fly without a plane."

"Are you really gonna find Makayla?"

Tanner laid a hand on Henry's shoulder. "I'll do the best I can. You have my word on that."

Henry moved forward and hugged him. "Thank you, oh God, thank you."

AFTER RETURNING INSIDE, LAURA FILLED THEM IN ON what had transpired between her and her ex-husband, Glenn.

"It was gambling. He was always a fanatic about playing the lottery, but then he began betting heavily on sports. I asked him to get counseling, but Glenn refused to see that he had a problem. Things fell apart after I learned he used Henry's college fund to bet on a football game. The thing is, he won, and won big, but he had signed my name in order to get to the money. That was the final straw for me, although it broke my heart to say goodbye to those girls of his. I thought we would always be a family."

"Where is Glenn now?" Sara asked.

"Oh, he moved west to Cincinnati. A cousin of his offered him a job there selling cars. He called me about six months ago and admitted he had lost everything while visiting Las Vegas. He asked if I thought we could make a go of it again. I said no, because I couldn't trust him."

"Trust is important," Sara agreed.

"I've been trying to keep this house in good shape, but it's difficult now that I've lost my old job and so I've decided to sell it."

"What sort of work did you do?" Tanner asked.

"Oh, right now, I'm an assistant manager at a retail store, but I used to be a dispatcher for a construction equipment company."

"Is that like a police dispatcher?"

"I guess it's similar, only they deal with

emergencies; I was just telling drivers what jobsite to go to."

"There's an opening in our town for one, a police dispatcher. The chief of police is a friend and he mentioned recently that the current dispatcher was retiring soon."

"You're friends with a cop?" Henry said.

Tanner smiled at the surprise in his voice. "He's one of my best friends."

"I keep an eye out for an opening in the field in this area," Laura said. "But so far I haven't had any luck."

Sara and Tanner stayed a little longer. Before leaving, Tanner made Henry a promise while they were alone.

"If I don't find Makayla, it won't be because I haven't done everything I can."

Henry smiled. "I feel better knowing you're looking for her. I mean the cops and the FBI are doing their best, but they don't play rough like the people they're after. A guy killed the two men who grabbed Makayla just because I saw their faces. People like that don't play by the rules."

"Neither do I," Tanner said.

After leaving Henry and Laura, Tanner drove Sara to the airport, then went in search of his next target, a man named Griffey.

MORE LINKS IN THE CHAIN

PITTSBURGH, PENNSYLVANIA

GRIFFEY WAS IVAN GRIFKOWSKI. HIS PARENTS immigrated to the United States from the Ukraine when Griffey was just seventeen months old.

Griffey had grown up in Pittsburgh then left home after high school to join the army. After six years of service spent mostly in Nebraska, he returned to his hometown. While he'd been gone, his best friend had become wealthy selling oxycontin. Meanwhile, Griffey didn't have a hundred dollars to his name. It didn't take him long to decide to join his friend's crew.

The friend looked out for him. Griffey didn't have to deal drugs himself. Instead, he was in charge of the guys who did. Griffey thought it was a great deal until one of the dealers was busted for possession and intent to distribute. It was the dealer's third such offense, and the prosecutor was looking to send him up for years. To get a lighter sentence, the punk gave Griffey up to the cops.

Griffey had a choice. He could hand his friend over to the police or take the rap and do hard time. Like the punk who had ratted him out, Griffey decided to talk. By doing so, he had taken eight years off his sentence. His friend was still doing time, although Griffey had been released years ago.

After having tasted easy money, Griffey wanted more of it. And since he had a criminal record and had served time, there weren't a lot of people looking to hire him.

He wanted to stay away from drugs. There were too many cops that had a hard-on for dealers. That was when he entered the sex trade and became a pornographer. He couldn't ever remember hearing about someone going to jail for selling smut, at least not during his lifetime.

Griffey rented an old house in the boondocks, then threw monthly parties where he would supply college kids with cheap booze and dope. Once their inhibitions were down, he'd introduce the element of sex. For that, Griffey paid a few hookers to get things rolling. By the end of the night, he'd have a wild sex tape he could sell or put up on the internet.

He made money, but it was nothing like the fat stacks he'd been pulling in while in the drug world. That was when Griffey was approached by a man who called himself Lion. Lion looked like a lion. He had a wild mane of hair, light brown skin, and eyes the color of amber.

Lion had heard about the parties Griffey set up for college kids and asked him if he wanted to make extra money.

Griffey only had one question. "How much money are we talking about?"

It was enough, and Griffey agreed to help. It was so simple. All Lion wanted Griffey to do was what he was already doing, taking pictures. Instead of filming only the women and girls who would get wild and join the fun, Lion wanted Griffey to concentrate on photographing any girls whom he considered a nine or better.

"You know, the really hot ones," Lion said. "And you'll need to find out where they live."

Griffey hired one of the guys he knew who used to sell drugs. Like Griffey, he had lost his taste for dealing. He had only done eighteen months in the can, but it had been enough.

His nickname was Trigger. If he had a real name, Griffey had never heard it. When he entered prison,

Trigger had been twenty-three but looked like a high school kid. When he came out less than two years later, he no longer resembled a teen. The beatings and degradation he'd suffered through had sapped the youth out of him. Life inside had been hard on Trigger's pretty-boy ass, literally.

Once Griffey found a particularly beautiful girl, he would have Trigger follow her. Within a month, Griffey had over a dozen names and addresses for Lion.

Several of those girls disappeared over the following year. The police feared there was a serial killer in the area. There wasn't. The women were still alive. They had been abducted, starved, sleep deprived, and conditioned into submission, then sold as sex slaves in Europe and the Middle East.

When Griffey realized what Lion was doing, he was shocked. It wasn't that he cared about what was happening to the young women he had targeted; no, he was angry that Lion was paying him so little to be involved. The son of a bitch was underpaying him. Griffey renegotiated his fee and hired more men like Trigger. He also recommended to Lion that he expand his territory.

"Dude, if the bitches around here keep disappearing, the heat is gonna get fierce. We need to take this shit on the road, there's a whole country full of hot ass girls out there."

Lion agreed and told Griffey to think of something. That was when Griffey came up with the idea of using a motor home. Trigger, or even better, a pair of guys, could travel around the country and find women. By using a motor home, it was less likely that a cop would pull them over. There would also be no record of them staying at motels in an area where girls went missing.

When the opportunity was right and a girl or a young woman could be grabbed up with no one watching, then she could be loaded into the RV and kept drugged.

Lion didn't like the idea because it would cost money. He didn't see that in the long run it would make them even more. It also cut down the possibility of someone catching on to them by abducting girls in a much wider area. No, Lion didn't like it, but *his* boss did, he was a man named Mr. Lennox.

Over the last few years, the motor home idea had worked great, while new people were recruited, and others lost. Lion was no longer around. He'd been killed in a car wreck after driving drunk on New Year's Eve of 2018.

Griffey had moved up into his slot. That didn't last long. For some reason, Mr. Lennox didn't like him. He brought in another guy to take Lion's place. He was a black guy called Armstrong. After that,

Griffey went back to making sex tapes and scouting out girls in the Pittsburgh area. The cops were still convinced that they were looking for a serial killer.

That was because every once in a while, Armstrong would kill a girl and leave her body somewhere that it would be found, like on a hiking trail. The sick bastard carved the letter A into their foreheads. The cops had nicknamed him the Scarlet Killer.

Armstrong thought it was funny. It was smart is what it was. Most of the girls they snatched and sold were of a type—long legs, good breasts, lots of hair, and pretty as hell. Many of them were listed as being victims of the serial killer. If they were ever busted for abducting or selling a girl, the cops would have a hard time pinning the earlier crimes on them. After all, it was assumed that they had been killed and dumped somewhere, as was the serial killer's M.O.

And then there was that shit that went down yesterday with Vernon and Sal. Not only did they come close to getting caught while grabbing a girl, but the teenager they took had a rich grandfather somewhere. Now the cops and the FBI were all juiced up to get the girl back.

Lennox had put the word out for everyone to lie low and not take any more girls. Sal and Vernon were dead, and Griffey knew it was Armstrong that killed them. They had fucked up, yeah, but damn, couldn't they have just been sent off somewhere for a while? They operated in eight states, Sal and Vernon could have just gone away and set up shop elsewhere.

Nope. They were dead, and it was a message to everyone else in the gang. Be cool, stay quiet, and wait for the storm to pass. Within a few days or a week, the press would forget about that girl Makayla and be hyping some other news story. By then, the girl would be overseas and someone else's problem.

Yeah, that was Griffey's plan. He was going to hang out in the casino, play some blackjack, and spend time with his girlfriend.

Griffey walked into the restaurant inside the casino where his girlfriend worked as a bartender. It was a quiet weeknight and there weren't many people around. There was a new face that Griffey took note of; it was a guy wearing jeans and a leather jacket, and damn if the dude didn't have some serious eyes.

BY THE WAY THE BARTENDER WAS SMILING AT THE GUY who'd entered and headed toward the bar, Tanner guessed he was looking at Griffey. He became more assured of that opinion when the bartender gave the man a kiss.

Decker's description of Griffey fit, right down to the goatee. He was a handsome man, although he gave off an aura that made Tanner think of a rat. Griffey's small eyes darted about the room and he looked as if he was ready to bolt at the first sign of trouble. When he had looked Tanner's way, those eyes had widened for an instant. Tanner glanced away first and looked down at his phone. He didn't want to scare Griffey away and have to chase him down. Every moment Makayla spent in the hands of her captives was a moment closer to disaster. If they didn't panic and kill her because of the heat that was coming down on them from the law, then she would be abused and sold off.

The bartender was good-looking, but not what Tanner expected. He figured anyone dating a scumbag like Griffey would be the hard-as-nails type. The woman tending bar had more of the manner of the girl next door. Maybe she had no idea what Griffey really did for a living.

Tanner finished the beer he'd been nursing, left a tip, then exited the bar. He sat at a slot machine that allowed him a view of Griffey. When it looked like he would have to be there for awhile, Tanner began feeding dollars into the machine.

Around midnight, Griffey and his girlfriend left the bar and headed for the parking lot. Tanner had won a little over a hundred dollars on the slots; he took it as a good omen although he didn't have time to cash in his winnings.

Assuming that Griffey would park by the nearest exit to the bar, Tanner had done the same. He saw Griffey open the door of a newer model BMW M5. The car was blue and glowed brilliantly beneath the parking lot lights. Tanner's black Jeep was five rows over from it. He started his engine and followed Griffey.

The couple arrived at an apartment house on Foster Street. The BMW disappeared into the building's underground parking garage and Tanner settled the Jeep in a spot where he could see the exit.

GRIFFEY LEFT HIS GIRLFRIEND'S APARTMENT AFTER only being inside for an hour. He never stayed the night. He was afraid that doing so might make his girlfriend, who was named Robin, get ideas. He liked Robin a lot but would never live with or marry anyone. There were just too many women in the world to ever settle for just one.

Besides, Robin thought he was a salesman. If they became serious, it would only be a matter of time until she figured out who and what he was. Despite having access to women in the sex trade, Griffey never dated any of them. He liked women who were… "normal."

Griffey climbed into his BMW and was about to hit the start button when a voice spoke from the rear seat.

"Let me see your hands."

Griffey jumped from fright. "Fuck!"

"I want to see those hands."

Griffey raised up his empty hands while looking into the rearview mirror. He recognized Tanner from earlier.

"You were in the bar. What is this?"

"The girl that was taken yesterday, Makayla Albertini, where is she being kept?"

"What? I don't know anything about that."

"If that's true, then you're useless to me. If you're useless, you're trash. You know what happens to trash."

"Trigger! There's a guy named Trigger."

"Is he your boss?"

"Yeah, and sometimes he watches the new girls for a few days until they can be shipped out."

"Where do I find him?"

"He has a house in the woods about twenty miles from here. I'll give you directions."

"I have a better idea," Tanner said.

An explosion of pain blossomed behind Griffey's

eyes as something hard slammed into the back of his head, and he felt himself passing out.

GRIFFEY CAME TO A FEW MINUTES LATER WHILE BEING slapped. He was sitting up in the rear of his car with his wrists and ankles bound by zip ties. Tanner had also buckled him into the seat and used more ties to fasten him to the seat belt.

"Oh, damn my head hurts. What did you hit me with?"

"You're going to give me directions to Trigger's house while I drive. Which way should I turn when we leave the garage?"

"What?"

Tanner slapped Griffey again. "Pay attention. Your life depends on it. How do I get to Trigger's house?"

"Um, turn right when you get out of here then make a left when you reach 44th Street. You'll be headed north after that."

Tanner started the engine and drove toward the exit. "Will I find Makayla there?"

"I don't know. You're not a cop, are you?"

"No."

"That kid, the one who was roughed up. He asked

somebody for help during the press conference…
that was you he was talking about?"

"That was me."

"Listen, even if you find the girl, the guy at the
top will send people after you."

"What's his name?"

"Mr. Lennox. I don't know his first name. He's
got a guy working for him named Armstrong. You
don't want Armstrong coming after you."

"It will be *me* going after him."

Griffey made a sound that was close to a laugh.
"You think you're a tough guy? Why would a tough
guy care about a punk kid and his girlfriend? You're
some friend of the family, right? Maybe you were in
the Marines or are some sort of special forces. That
shit won't matter. Mr. Lennox can hire a dozen
guys to come after you, and hey dude, when they
find you, they'll kill you and anybody who's with
you."

"What do Armstrong and Lennox look like?"

"Why should I tell you?"

"Because if you don't, I'll break your knees. And
if you give me bad descriptions, when I find out I'll
come back and break your neck."

Griffey swallowed hard before speaking again.
"Armstrong is a black guy with a shaved head. He's
about six feet tall and muscular. His eyes aren't as
weird as yours, but the dude can stare you down

every time. I bet he's the one who killed Sal and Vernon. Armstrong is one cold dude."

"And what about Lennox?"

Griffey shrugged. "I've never seen him. The only time I've been around him he was seated in the back of a white limo with tinted windows. I bet the only one who's ever seen him is Armstrong, and oh yeah, this guy named Lion might have seen Lennox, but Lion is dead."

"Is Makayla the only girl they have?"

"Hell no. This is a big business and we operate in more than one state. I bet we sell a couple of hundred girls a year, maybe even more."

TANNER REACHED THE HOUSE WHERE GRIFFEY SAID Trigger lived. He was on foot, having parked some distance from the home. It looked familiar and he realized it resembled the abandoned house where Henry had been found. They had showed video of that place on the news, including an aerial view.

This home was in better shape but had a large detached garage like the other house had. There was the glow of diffused light leaking out around windows in the garage that had been painted over, and wood smoke drifted up from a vent pipe.

Tanner had rendered Griffey unconscious with a

strong dose of a sedative. He had asked Duke for a supply of the drug in case it was needed.

If all worked out well, he would be leading Makayla and possibly other girls to safety. It would be understandable if they were traumatized or in emotional distress over what they'd been through. Sara had suggested that a sedative might be needed if one of them became distraught. Tanner would have a difficult enough time rescuing the girls, he didn't need to have to fight while worried about Makayla or some other girl freaking out.

There was only one vehicle in sight. It was an old Cadillac that had seen better days. Tanner moved past the car to head toward the rear of the house. There were no signs of cameras or alarms. The house was surrounded by other homes but separated by woods. They were all spread out with the nearest one being a quarter of a mile away.

While looking through a gap in a window blind, Tanner viewed the kitchen. There was no one in it but the light was on. It took only seconds to pick the lock on the back door and enter. The place smelled of old beer. The odor was coming from a recycling bin that was in a corner of the room. It was full of empty beer cans and more were piled in a cardboard carton beside it.

It took Tanner a few minutes to roam the house and determine that it was empty. After unlocking the front door, he moved outside and headed for the garage.

TRIGGER WAS IN THE GARAGE MOPPING UP THE FLOOR. He had been glad when Armstrong called him and said that he was to chill for a few days until the heat died down. It gave him a chance to spend some time working on a side project. He had been looking for ways to earn more money and an idea had occurred to him.

Armstrong usually gave him four to six girls a month to keep an eye on. It was Trigger's job to "condition" them for their new life as sex slaves. That didn't mean he got to screw them, hell no. If Armstrong ever caught him raping one of the girls, he would rip his balls off with his bare hands.

No, all Trigger had to do was tell the girls the new facts of life. They would never be found, would wind up in a foreign country, and if they didn't do as they were told, well, there was no shortage of girls.

He wasn't supposed to feed them unless they behaved, which was fine by him. That usually meant that they didn't get anything to eat for the first day or two. They were locked up in dog cages that weren't big enough to stand up in and they could only lie down if they bent their legs.

Bright lights and blaring music kept the girls from being able to fall asleep. When it was cold, the heat was turned off, and when it was hot, they received no air-conditioning.

A lot of the girls were making threats the first day and begging for mercy by the third night. Some offered to sleep with Trigger. As hot as they were, after they'd spent three days in a cage without a bathroom or a shower, he didn't find it difficult to pass on their offers. Once they were cleaned up and ready to be shipped out, that changed and he was tempted, but then he would remember Armstrong and keep it in his pants.

It wasn't a bad job all in all. He even felt sorry for the girls sometimes. Hell, when he was in prison, he'd been raped nearly every day. Although they were locked up, at least these girls didn't have to go through that. Then again, once they arrived at the home of the men who paid for them, they would be raped. That was the kind of world it was. You were either the fucker or the fuckee.

Trigger's idea to make more money was simple. He would take pictures of the girls when he had them in the cage. Once they were gone and couldn't be traced, he would contact their parents online and show them a photo. Sort of a proof of life thing, like kidnappers used.

Once they saw the photo, the girl's parents would

be ready to pay him anything to see more or find out where their daughter was. There were a couple of problems with his plan. For one, Trigger couldn't figure out how to get paid.

He couldn't meet with the parents and get the money in person, or give them a bank account to deposit the money in. If he did that, the cops would be all over him. No, but there must be a way to do it that was safe. Another problem was Armstrong. If he ever found out that Trigger was risking being caught by shaking down the girls' parents, he would plant Trigger in a hole somewhere. Because of that, a system had to be found to keep everything out of the news.

Now that he had some time off, Trigger would use it to think of a way to get paid and not have anyone else know about it. In the meantime, it was also a good opportunity to clean the cages and the rest of the garage. The place stank. He once asked Armstrong if he could place buckets in the cages so the girls would have something to piss in. The answer had been no.

Trigger thought that maybe Armstrong hated women. Not that he thought he was gay or anything like that. Maybe Armstrong just hated. Period.

Trigger was startled when a noise came from behind him and he saw the side door in the barn opening up. That door had been locked. A man stepped through. He was dressed in jeans and a leather jacket. When he raised his right hand, Trigger saw the gun. The sound suppressor screwed onto the end of it made the weapon appear huge.

"I ain't got no money, dude."

The man rushed toward him and shoved him to the floor. Trigger felt his pants grow damp. He was sitting on a spot he'd just mopped with diluted bleach.

"This isn't a robbery," Tanner told him. "I'm looking for Makayla Albertini."

"Who?"

Tanner sent a kick between Trigger's legs. "The girl who was snatched from the parking lot of a restaurant yesterday. Where is she?"

Trigger couldn't speak until a wave of pain and nausea passed. While that was happening, Tanner patted him down. He didn't have a gun, only a cell phone, wallet, and keys, which Tanner pocketed. Once he was recovered enough, Trigger asked a question.

"You're not a cop. Who are you?"

"Where's Makayla? And don't tell me you don't know what I'm talking about."

"All right, but I don't know where she is. She sure as shit ain't here. She was supposed to come here, but that got changed."

"Who made the change, Lennox?"

"How do you know about Mr. Lennox?"

"Just tell me where I can find him."

"Me? I've never even seen Lennox. The only one I see is Armstrong, and the others."

"What others? Give me their names."

"There's these two mean-looking assholes. I don't know their names and they don't ever talk to me. I just think of them as the musclemen because they're the bodybuilder type. Then there's Gramps and Granny."

"What do you mean?"

"An old couple, only they're not married or anything. Armstrong always calls them Gramps and Granny."

"They're part of the gang?"

"They drive an RV, a big one. That's how we move the girls around in this area. Gramps looks like the grandpa type and so he never gets pulled over by the cops."

"How do I find them?"

"Hell if I know. How did you find me?"

"Griffey sent me here. He said you were his boss."

Trigger cursed. "I ain't his boss. I'm just another worker bee like he is. Hell, if anything, he's my boss."

Tanner looked around. "You keep the girls locked in these cages?"

Trigger tried to smile. "No, I ah, I used to have dogs, but they died."

"Get inside a cage."

"Hell no."

"Get inside a cage or I'll kick you unconscious and shove you into one of them."

"Those cages are small."

"In the cage, now."

Trigger complied. He made it to his feet and walked over to one of the cages. Unfortunately for him, he had yet to clean them. They stank of urine and dried feces. Trigger lowered himself to the floor and backed into the cage. Once he was inside, Tanner shut the door and engaged the padlock hanging on it. It was the type that opened with a key.

"This is...what's the word, inhumane?" Trigger said.

"You're right, and how many girls have you locked up in there?"

"I'm not saying another word. You ain't a cop and I don't have to talk to you."

Tanner took aim and sent a bullet between one of the two-inch squares of the wire cage. The slug tore through the outer portion of Trigger's left biceps and exited out the rear of the cage. His howl of agony was loud. No one would hear it. The garage had been soundproofed.

Tanner let him adjust to the pain before continuing. "I need a name or a location where I can find the people you mentioned."

"Oh God almighty, look what you did to my arm."

"Tell me where to find them, Trigger."

"I don't know. It's not like we're friends. They come here, drop off the girls and leave."

"In a motor home?"

"Yeah."

"Do the bodybuilders live on it with the older man and woman?"

"Shit, my arm hurts, and it won't stop bleeding."

Tanner grabbed a towel from a stack that was sitting on a shelf. They were the towels the abducted girls used to dry off whenever Trigger blasted a garden hose at them to clean them up.

"Press that against the wound, then forget your arm and tell me something I can use. If not, I'll shoot you again."

"Did you torture Griffey like this? It's no wonder he gave you my name."

"Tell me something I can use."

"I don't know anything! All I ever—wait! The musclemen, they're always wearing shirts that have the name of a bar on it. It's the Eighth Street Bar in Altoona."

"Altoona? Have you been there?"

"No, but those guys must live there given how many T-shirts and hoodies they have with the name on it."

"Can you think of anything else?"

Trigger looked up with tears in his eyes. "All I can think of is how much my arm hurts."

Tanner turned and headed for the door.

Trigger shouted after him. "Hey man, let me out of this cage. If you leave me like this I might not be found for a month."

"You may be right," Tanner said. He opened the door and shut it behind him. Trigger's desperate plea to be released was silenced by the soundproofing.

Tanner had another location to check out and two more links in the chain to rattle. He was getting closer to Makayla. He just hoped she could hang on.

10

MYSTERY MAN

HENRY AND HIS GRANDMOTHER, LAURA, SHARED A look of surprise as they heard the sound of a car traveling up their graveled driveway. It was late, and although they'd been up watching a movie, they were both wearing robes and were planning to go to sleep.

Laura headed to the peephole in the door as Henry grabbed his rifle. When Laura announced who their visitors were, Henry relaxed and placed the rifle out of sight.

"It's that FBI agent Kyle Croft, and two other agents."

"I hope this means they've found Makayla."

Croft apologized for the late visit, then introduced the other two agents, who were a man and a woman. By the way they hung back and only nodded, it appeared that Croft would do most of the talking.

"Have you rescued Makayla?" Henry asked.

"No, Henry, I'm sorry to say that we haven't. I'm actually here on another matter."

"What could be more important than finding Makayla?"

"That is our priority, but you may have complicated matters."

"Me? What did I do?"

The woman agent spoke up. She was a little older than Croft and wore a stern expression.

"During the press conference you begged someone to help find your girlfriend. It appears as if he's agreed to do so. What we want to know is, how long have you been in contact with him?"

Henry fought to maintain his calm. He hadn't meant to get Cody in trouble, but it was looking like the FBI was on his trail.

"I haven't been in contact with anyone… I was just asking for help, you know, from the public."

The woman smiled; it was not a pleasant smile. "You know where he is, don't you?"

Laura held up her hands. "What are you talking about?"

"Henry's father, Ms. Knight," Croft said. "We need to know how long Henry has been in contact with him."

"What? No! That's not possible. That man has been out of our lives since Henry was a baby."

"I've read the file. I know what went on years ago. You lived through it; you know how dangerous the man is. If you know anything you need to tell us now."

"I don't know anything, and I would never let him back into Henry's life. Henry has never seen him or even knows his name." Laura looked at Henry with uncertainty. "Have you?"

Henry shook his head. "No, but it sounds like you know more about my father than what you've been telling me. Who is he, Grandma? What did he do that has the FBI looking for him?"

Laura turned away from Henry and spoke to the agents. "We don't know anything about—the man you're looking for. My grandson was nearly killed yesterday and now you're harassing us."

Croft raised his hands in a calming gesture. "We came here looking for answers. Henry did make a plea for help and we have reason to believe that someone outside law enforcement may have acted to locate Makayla."

"What reason?"

"A man has been killed. His name was Vincent Decker. Authorities in New Jersey had been building a case against him for running a prostitution ring; there was also evidence to suggest that he was involved in sex trafficking. After receiving that tip, agents in New Jersey went to Decker's home to question him. They arrived to find a homicide cop on the scene investigating Decker's murder."

"They think he was involved in Makayla's abduction?"

"No, but he may have known someone who was. Now, we'll never know what he knew."

Henry had to keep himself from smiling. Tanner had killed Decker, and Henry was certain that he'd made the man talk before doing so. Agent X was on the case.

Croft called to Henry, snapping him out of his reverie.

"Yes, sir?" Henry said.

"We know you were addressing someone in particular when you spoke to the press. If it wasn't your father, who is this mystery man?"

"What's my father's name? I don't even know his name."

Croft glanced over at Laura. "Given your age, I'll let your grandmother decide how much you should know. And you haven't answered my question."

"I don't have to answer. I did what I did to help Makayla. All I care about is having someone find Makayla. You're wasting time talking to me."

The female agent pointed at Henry. "Maybe we should take you in for a more formal discussion."

"Do it if you want to; I still won't tell you anything."

"You can't arrest him," Laura said. "My grandson was a victim. Maybe I should be talking to a lawyer."

"Don't bother," Croft said. "We're leaving. But Henry, we'll be back if anything else happens. Whoever you were talking to can't be allowed to interfere in the investigation."

Henry said nothing else. After the agents left and were driving away, Laura turned from the door.

"You asked for help in finding Makayla and Cody Parker appeared. He was also here the day before Boyd Kessler, I mean, Brock Kessler went missing."

Henry looked down at the floor. Laura walked over to him and raised his chin.

"Did Cody do something to the man who killed your mother?"

Henry nodded.

Laura's lips parted in surprise. "Brock Kessler didn't run off to hide, did he?"

"No, Grandma. He paid for killing Mom."

Laura embraced Henry in a hug. "It sounds like I owe Cody Parker for avenging my baby's death. He may have also saved our lives by getting rid of that fiend."

"He'll find Makayla too."

"Oh honey, that's easier said than done."

"Not for Cody."

Laura kissed her grandson on the cheek. "I don't know about you, but I'm exhausted. Let's get some sleep."

"All right, but don't tell anyone what I said about Cody."

"I don't plan to."

"Do you plan on telling me about my father?"

Laura's face creased into a pained expression. "Maybe when you're a little older."

"I'm not a kid anymore, Grandma."

"Yes. I figured that out when I came home early and found you and Makayla in bed together."

Henry smiled, even as he reddened a shade. He then moaned.

"Makayla has to be found. Oh God, if only I could have beaten the two men who took her at the restaurant."

"Henry, I know you think you're grown but you're still a boy, and they were two men with a gun. You were lucky they didn't kill you."

"I still feel like I let Makayla down."

"You didn't. There aren't many men who could have done more than you did, even if they had training."

Henry nodded. Training, yes, he needed training. He never wanted to feel helpless ever again.

11

JUST ANOTHER DAY AT THE OFFICE

IN A SMALL TOWN NORTHEAST OF PITTSBURGH, Armstrong sat in the kitchen of a house making calls. He had learned that Vince Decker had been killed earlier and thought nothing of it at first. However, something about the death nagged at him. When he remembered that Decker occasionally sold girls to his man Griffey, he decided to give Griffey a call.

There was no answer, as Griffey's phone went to voicemail. A short time later when Trigger also didn't pick up, Armstrong felt a tingle along his spine. Something was wrong, very wrong. Neither one of those men would ignore a call from him. That meant they couldn't answer, maybe it meant they were dead.

When he asked himself who would be making a

move on them, all he could think of was one of the gangs they sold the girls to. They were a Columbian street gang with contacts in the Middle East. They sold the girls to the Columbians for cash, then the gang traded the girls to their contacts for heroin and opium. Once the drugs were sold, they had more cash to buy girls.

Armstrong wondered if the leader of the gang, a swarthy man named Alejandro, was thinking of cutting him out and taking over his operation. He placed a call to the man and spoke with him for a while. There was no fear of waking him. Alejandro wasn't the early-to-bed, early-to-rise type. When they discussed the girl Sal and Vernon had grabbed, the gang leader asked when Armstrong would be selling her. He sounded normal to Armstrong and not like he was hiding anything.

"I have to wait until some other big news or crime grabs the cops' attention before I risk moving the girls. When things cool down, we'll pay you a visit. Right now, we've got six girls."

"What was that shit that chico was talking about at the press conference?"

"You mean the boyfriend?"

"Yeah. He was asking someone to help find his girl. Does the boy have a relative in the CIA or something?"

Armstrong ran a hand over his shaved head. "I

don't know. But you're right, that was odd. I'll call again when things are back to normal."

"Why wait, amigo? Bring us the bitches and we'll have them on a ship by this time tomorrow."

"It's tempting, but the law is looking hard for this girl. I don't want to take a chance of getting stopped on the highway."

"In that motor home, with the old farts driving? The cops would just wave them through a checkpoint."

"Maybe, but soon they won't be looking for her at all."

"Yeah, okay. Later, Armstrong."

After the call, Armstrong went online and watched the press conference again. He fast-forwarded to the part where Henry made his impassioned plea.

"...If that man is listening... I'm begging you, please help me again. I... I love Makayla. Please find her. If anyone can do it, I know you can."

Maybe that man was listening, boy. And maybe you've sent a world of trouble my way.

Armstrong made another call. The tension in his shoulders relaxed as it was answered on the third ring.

"Eighth Street Bar."

"Is this Benny or Gary?"

"It's Benny, Mr. Armstrong."

"Benny, there's been trouble. A guy named Decker was killed and I can't get Griffey or Trigger on the phone."

"You think it's the cops?"

"The cops wouldn't have killed a guy and walked away from it. No, this is something else. You and Gary get ready for trouble; I think it's headed your way."

"How many guys are we talking about?"

"If it's what I think it is, it's just one guy."

"One guy? If that's true, we'll handle him easy, especially now that we're expecting him."

"I know it's getting late but call me every two hours. And listen, if you can grab this guy up instead of killing him there's two thousand each for you."

"I like that, and I'll tell Gary what's going on."

"Don't forget, call me every two hours."

"Right, Mr. Armstrong."

The call ended. Armstrong left the kitchen and walked into the living room. The old man everyone called Gramps was still up and watching a movie. Granny was asleep on the sofa beside him with her legs curled up under her. She had drunk half a bottle of wine as they were watching television and it put her lights out. When he saw Armstrong enter the room, Gramps muted the TV.

"When was the last time you checked on the girls?" Armstrong asked.

"About two hours ago. Not one of them is giving us shit anymore, but that Makayla girl asked me about her boyfriend again. She thinks Sal and Vernon killed him."

"What did you tell her?"

"I told her to keep her bitch mouth shut before I shut it for her."

"Good, don't tell her shit. If she thinks the kid is dead maybe she'll behave."

"One of the other girls offered to let me do anything I wanted to her if I'd let her go."

Armstrong smiled. "How many times have you had that offer?"

"I can't count that high."

"Did you enlist her?"

"I sure did. I had Granny free her from the cage and we took her into the house and let her use the bathroom, then gave her some food. I told her the deal. If she let us know what the other girls were saying she'd continue to get special treatment."

"Good. It never hurts to have a snitch among the girls. That was how we found out that bitch had a knife hidden on her a couple of years ago."

"I promised her we'd let her go if she stopped anyone from breaking out, even though there's not much chance of any of them getting out of those cages."

"That's a bigger risk than usual. There's been some trouble, but Benny and Gary will handle it."

"Cops?"

"No, just some asshole do-gooder looking to rescue that Makayla girl."

Gramps smiled. "That kid, the one that beat the shit out of Ray and Vernon. He's sicced someone on us, didn't he?"

"I think so. The guy might have killed one of our contacts."

"Who?"

"Vince Decker."

"Decker? Oh, in Jersey, right?"

"Yeah. He ran girls in AC."

"He's dead. How did he get it?"

"Shot in his own house."

"That's serious. I hope Benny and Gary don't have any trouble they can't handle."

"They shouldn't. I'd feel better though if I knew who it was we were dealing with."

Gramps smiled. "That kid knows who it is."

Armstrong smiled back at him. "He does, doesn't he?"

BENNY AND GARY DIDN'T HANG OUT IN THE EIGHTH Street bar as Trigger had assumed; they owned the place. With trouble on the way, they made an excuse to their regulars and closed up early to prepare.

TANNER ARRIVED IN THE AREA AFTER LEAVING Trigger in the cage. It was past midnight and the streets of Altoona were quieting down on a late Monday evening. Tanner had driven past the bar and noted that it was dark; however, there appeared to be lights on at the rear. It was too early for a bar to be closed, even on a weekday. It made Tanner wonder if he had lost the element of surprise.

It didn't matter. If the two musclemen were there, they were the next links in the chain that led to finding Makayla. Trigger said they had a connection to the bar, so it had to be checked out. Tanner parked Griffey's BMW and made preparations.

THE TWO MUSCLEMEN, BENNY AND GARY, STARED AT a laptop and watched via a security camera as a figure approached the back door of the bar. They'd left the lights on in the office to make it look like they were in there, then concealed themselves behind a leather sofa. When someone knocked on the door, they gave each other surprised looks. They had been expecting the door to be kicked in or have the lock picked.

Benny sent Gary a shrug and called out. "Who is it?"

"It's Griffey. Let me in, it's cold out here."

A check of the laptop revealed that Griffey was alone. Benny and Gary popped up from behind the sofa and opened the door for Griffey. He walked in and shut the door behind him.

"What the hell are you doing here?" Benny asked him. "Mr. Armstrong thought you were dead."

Griffey stared at the two men, saw their weapons, and showed them his empty hands.

"I was grabbed up by this guy and brought here. He sent me in to tell you he wants to make a deal."

"What sort of deal?"

"Who the hell cares? There are three of us now. I say we go outside and kill him."

"Why are you talking funny? Are you drunk?" Gary asked.

"He drugged me with something. It's made me a little loopy."

Griffey was still dazed from the drug Tanner had given him. When his phone rang, he took it out and stared at it.

"This isn't my phone. It's way thicker than mine."

The phone kept ringing, so Griffey answered it. "Hello?"

"It's me," Tanner said. "Are the two bodybuilder types there?"

"Yeah, they're here."

"Are they alone?"

"That's right. Why don't you come on in so we can talk."

"I'll be right there."

Griffey stared at the phone after Tanner ended the call. "He said he's coming in."

There was a loud blast of noise and a burst of intense light as the phone in Griffey's hand exploded.

The cell phones Duke had given Tanner were disguised flash-bang grenades. The grenade went off and stunned all three men while seriously injuring Griffey. Part of the phone's plastic casing had punctured his throat and nicked an artery.

Tanner entered the office and locked the door behind him. Benny and Gary were still affected by the blast and Tanner had no trouble disarming them.

Griffey was on the floor with blood spreading around him. Most of the blood came from his throat but he was also missing a finger on the hand that had been gripping the phone. Tanner made a mental note to ask Duke to order more of the explosive cell phones.

Tanner told Benny and Gary to stand and head out into the bar. After turning on the lights, it was plain to see that there was no one else in the small pub. Tanner closed the curtains across the front windows. They were there to keep the glare out in the daytime and would work just as well to provide a little privacy.

Just to be safe, and thorough, Tanner herded the men at gunpoint toward the restrooms so he could check them out. Once he was satisfied that the restrooms were empty, he had the two bodybuilders return up front and lean back against the bar.

Gary decided to be tough and told Tanner to go to hell.

"We aren't saying shit, asshole."

Tanner used his silenced pistol to send two rounds into Gary's chest; one of the rounds pierced his heart and Gary dropped to the floor as if he were boneless.

The remaining man, Benny, looked down at his friend's body with disbelieving eyes.

"Talk or die," Tanner said. "That's your only choice."

Benny pointed down at Gary's body. "We were friends since the second grade... and you snuffed him out just like that."

"The girls you and your dead buddy grab up all

have friends, and parents, brothers and sisters. You never gave a damn about them, did you?"

Benny sniffled and wiped his face with a sleeve. "What the fuck do you want?"

"I think you know since you were expecting me."

"Yeah, we were expecting you. Armstrong knows you want the girl, but he'll never give her to you and you'll never find her."

"Do you know where he is?"

"I think so."

"Will Lennox be there too?"

"Mr. Lennox never gets his hands dirty and he only deals with Mr. Armstrong."

"So I've heard. Where can I find Armstrong?"

"Will you let me live if I tell you?"

"I'll let you live if you lead me to him."

Benny released a sigh. "I guess I'll have to take your word on that."

"My word is good. I gave my word that I would find Makayla and I intend to do it."

"Okay, but Mr. Armstrong may have moved to somewhere I don't know."

"What do you know? Do you know where I can find the old couple?"

"Gramps and Granny? Yeah, I know where they could be, and Mr. Armstrong should be there too."

Benny went on to tell Tanner about a town that was northeast of Pittsburgh.

"You're going to give me directions there when we get to the car."

"There's a chance that your girl has been sold already."

"Who would be the buyer?"

Benny told Tanner about the Columbian street gang that was lined up to buy the girls. "Maybe Armstrong is meeting with Alejandro right now to sell the girl and be done with her."

"Where do I find them?"

Benny laughed. "I'll tell you, no problem. There's about two dozen of those assholes. If you go there, they'll carve you up and use you for fish bait."

"Fish bait?"

"They're up at an old lodge near Lake Erie, Kroger Lodge. The place caught fire a few years back and the gang took it over. If Armstrong drove the girl there, you might as well kiss her goodbye."

"We'll check out the old couple first," Tanner said. "If Makayla isn't there, then I'll deal with the gang."

As he spoke, he had been looking through Benny's phone. Someone called the phone frequently from a local number. Tanner suspected it might be Armstrong.

"One more thing before we go," Benny said. "Mr. Armstrong mentioned that if you got past us, he was going to send you a message. I don't think it's a message you would want to hear."

"Maybe I'll get to him first. Let's go."

"Let me say goodbye to Gary."

Benny bent down and touched his friend on the shoulder while lowering his head as if he were praying. From the crouch, he sprang backwards and landed atop the bar, then dropped behind it and out of sight.

Tanner dived to the floor and sent a flurry of shots through the bar. There was the sound of shattering glass, then a cry of pain from Benny. There was also the thud of something heavy hitting the floor. It sounded like it was made of metal.

Tanner moved with caution to check on Benny. He saw that Benny had been going for a shotgun that was behind the bar. The big man sat with his back against a rack of bottles, with some leaking their contents onto him. Benny was leaking worse. There were two wounds in his chest. They were almost in the same spot where Tanner had shot Gary. The wounded bodybuilder gazed up at him with blood dribbling from a corner of his mouth. He didn't have long to live.

Thanks to his attempt to get revenge for his friend's death, Tanner had never found out where Gramps and Granny made their home. The town Benny said they lived in had over six thousand residents.

Tanner left Benny to die and headed to Lake Erie.

Maybe the Columbian street gang would prove useful.

Benny said there were two dozen members in the gang. Most men would never think of going up against such odds while alone. For Tanner, it was just another day at the office.

MESSAGE RECEIVED; MESSAGE SENT

ARMSTRONG WAS BACK IN THE KITCHEN. IT LOOKED like it was going to be a long night and he was on his fourth cup of coffee.

When Benny failed to call and no one answered at the bar, Armstrong realized he had a bigger problem than he'd imagined. Benny and Gary had been prepared and the man who was searching for Makayla still got the best of them. Maybe it was more than one man. If so, precautions had to be taken.

Armstrong sent off an email to an acquaintance who hired out muscle. He wrote that he needed five men, deleted that, and changed the request to ten, then made it an even dozen. Hiring a dozen trained, armed men was expensive, but too few men could wind up costing him his life.

In the living room, Granny was stirring from her nap just in time to go to bed. She looked to be the grandmotherly type and one could easily picture her making cookies for a brood of apple-cheeked youngsters. Few knew that she had been a porn actress in the seventies and a hooker until she hit fifty. Armstrong told her that he needed her to do one more thing before she went to bed.

"What's that?"

"Bring me a girl."

TANNER WAS HEADED NORTH ON I-79 WHEN SARA called him with the news. The body of a teen girl had been dumped at a bus stop in Pittsburgh. Reporters were speculating that it was Makayla Albertini.

Tanner pulled over to the side of the road. "How long ago was this?"

"I think it just happened. I checked the news on my phone as I was about to go to sleep and saw the report. Oh, for Henry's sake, I pray it's not her."

"So do I," Tanner said.

Benny had told Tanner that Armstrong was planning to send him a message. It appeared he had done so. If Armstrong believed that Tanner would stop with Makayla's death, he was wrong.

Murdering Makayla would only increase Tanner's desire to eliminate the people who'd harmed her.

TANNER READ A NEWS UPDATE ON HIS PHONE MINUTES after the call with Sara ended. The girl found murdered was not Makayla. She was a different teen named Sandra Owens who it was believed had run away from home three days earlier in Ohio, before Makayla's abduction. She bore a superficial resemblance to Makayla mostly due to her long auburn hair.

A reporter interviewed the cab driver who'd found the body. He said that words had been carved onto the teen's forehead. There were two words —BACK OFF!

Armstrong's message had been received. Tanner figured he owed the man a reply.

KROGER LODGE HAD BEEN BUILT IN THE FORTIES AND became a favorite destination for duck hunters. It had fallen out of favor with sportsmen and tourists in the Lake Erie region when newer, larger, and more modern hotels were built nearby. The property passed through several hands over the years, then was foreclosed on after a fire damaged part of the building.

The area's homeless squatted inside for a short time before being chased off by Alejandro and his gang. The bank that owned the property had it listed for sale at a price few were willing to pay. Those in charge knew that, while the building wasn't worth much, the land was. When the right buyer came along, most likely a property developer with deep pockets, there would be profit to be had.

In the meantime, the Columbians used the old lodge as a headquarters when they were in the area. They kept their motorcycles and pickup trucks out of sight of the road and were seldom hassled by the police. Whenever a cop did show up, the gang would leave for a few days, then return. The last time it occurred, Alejandro had found that a bribe to the right man made the problem go away. It had been months since they'd had to leave, and the old lodge was beginning to feel like home.

Water still flowed through the plumbing, thanks to a well, but electricity was provided by a generator the gang kept running. Heat was becoming a problem now that winter was in the air, but a wood burning stove warmed up the kitchen, which was where most of the gang hung out during the day. At night, they made do with sleeping bags and mounds of blankets.

ALEJANDRO WAS A SQUAT BUT POWERFULLY BUILT MAN in his twenties. He had grown up in a good home in Bogota but was always getting into trouble with the law. He joined the gang after quitting school and proved to be ruthless and daring. He loved the life of an outlaw and broke all contact with his family.

It had been only a year earlier that he became the leader of the gang after the prior man in charge was convicted of drug smuggling. The previous leader had been foolish. When arrested he was carrying his favorite gun, a Springfield P9. He had kept the weapon despite having used it to commit three murders. When the ballistic report came back, homicide charges were leveled against him and he was later sentenced to thirty years without parole.

Alejandro liked being in charge. It suited him, as he had never taken well to being ordered around. He was angry that the delivery of Makayla and the rest of the girls was being delayed. He'd had plans to ship the girls out and then head south to Florida for several weeks. They didn't know anyone down there who trafficked girls, but they occasionally acted as drug mules for one of the Mexican cartels. Being from a country that sat near the equator, Alejandro was no fan of the cold. He wanted to make one more deal with Armstrong then leave Pennsylvania until spring. Instead, he was looking at spending as much as a week more shivering his ass off at night.

A woman would have been nice to have for sex and warmth. His old lady was in Florida waiting for him, and likely up to no good if he knew her as well as he thought he did.

Alejandro checked the time by looking at his phone. He was alone in the kitchen. It was nearly four a.m. and the fire was dying in the stove. He tossed in another small log and headed for his room to climb into bed.

Since they were in a lodge, they each had their own room. Being jefe, Alejandro's room had a small heater inside it that was connected to the generator by a series of extension cords. It made the room comfortable once you burrowed beneath a few blankets. Even so, the tip of Alejandro's nose was always cold when he woke up.

After draining what was left of a bottle of wine, Alejandro climbed atop the bed and went to sleep. Outside, Tanner was preparing to commit wholesale slaughter.

Tanner had been observing the lodge for over an hour. When he'd arrived, there had been a group of three gang members sitting around a fire pit and cleaning their guns while talking in Spanish. The talk had been about the delay in receiving the girls and how, like Alejandro, they were looking forward to going south.

One of them mentioned that Armstrong wouldn't be arriving for six or seven days. Tanner couldn't wait that long, so he decided to send Armstrong a message of his own.

Alejandro had been the last man awake. After the lights went out in the kitchen, Tanner waited twenty minutes before breaking into the lodge by shattering a window. Any noise he made was covered up by the loud motor of the nearby generator.

He explored the lower level of the lodge with his gun leading the way. He found a grand but dated lobby, a large kitchen and pantry, and storage rooms and office space. All the guest rooms were on the top three floors. During his surveillance, Tanner had only spotted the glow of battery-powered lanterns through windows on the second floor.

Dawn was still over an hour away when he crept up the stairs, and as he moved, death strode with him.

THE FIRST MAN TO DIE DID SO WITHOUT KNOWING IT was happening. He was drunk off cheap whiskey and a sound sleeper. Tanner had knelt beside his sleeping bag, judged from the position of his bearded chin where his heart would be, and gave the knife he was gripping a downward thrust. The blade was twelve inches of surgically sharp steel. It went through the sleeping bag, the man's clothing, and his flesh, finding no more resistance than if they'd been warm butter.

The gang member's eyes never opened as his body shuddered and breath was expelled. Tanner placed a hand atop the bag and felt no movement. After wiping the knife clean on the side of the sleeping bag, he moved like a shadow to the next room.

Man number two had been drinking but wasn't drunk. His eyes flickered open as Tanner stood over him. Tanner clamped a hand over his mouth. At the same time, he sliced open the man's throat.

The eighth man had placed empty beer cans in front of his door in the shape of a pyramid. Tanner had looked beneath the door before entering and seen the base of the structure. If he attempted to open the door, the cans would fall and make a racket.

There had been no cans by the window. Unlike its modern counterparts, the Kroger Lodge had actual working windows that could be raised or lowered. Tanner put one to use. After patiently spending ten minutes easing the window open, he killed the architect of the beer can pyramid.

TANNER WAS BEING AS QUIET AS HE COULD AS HE entered the room belonging to the fourteenth man. It hadn't prevented a floorboard from making a noise as he placed his weight on it. A form in a sleeping bag was lying atop a bed. He woke and stared at Tanner with bleary eyes. Tanner considered using the silenced pistol then nixed the idea. While much quieter than an ordinary weapon, the gun was not silent. If he fired it inside the confines of a room, the noise wouldn't go unheard by those still alive.

The knife was flung as the man was opening his mouth to cry out. The blade stifled his voice and caused him to gag on his own blood. Tanner silenced the thug by breaking his neck.

The sound of movement could be heard in the hallway moments later. The gagging sounds had been overheard. There came a tap at the door. It was followed by a voice speaking in hushed tones.

"Ernesto? You okay, amigo? I heard noises coming from in here."

When there was no reply, the door opened and a man wearing a pair of red briefs walked in.

"Ernesto?"

The dead man didn't answer. Tanner had turned the body so that the rear of the sleeping bag was facing the door. Ernesto's concerned friend took three more steps toward the bed but froze as he sensed movement behind him. He had sensed it a little too late.

ALEJANDRO WOKE UP AS THE SOUND OF THE HEATER ceased. Still sleepy, he lay there with his eyes closed and wondered if the generator had run out of gas again.

When he realized he could still hear the steady grinding hum of the machine in the distance, he wondered why the heater had quit and turned over to take a look at it. Instead of the heater, he saw the outline of a man holding a gun. Given the length of the barrel, he assumed it had a silencer on it. Night was fleeing as a new day dawned, but the sun had only just begun its ascent. The man with the gun was still more shadow than substance.

As the veil of sleep was replaced by an elevated pulse, Alejandro became aware of something else. It was an odor, a strong scent, one he knew but had yet to identify.

After cursing in Spanish, Alejandro asked a question in English. "What is this about?"

"It's about a girl named Makayla," Tanner said.

Alejandro cursed again. "That little puta has been more trouble than she's worth. Are you law?"

"Not law," Tanner said, and it was at that moment that the sun peeked over the trees in the east, increasing the illumination in the room and causing Alejandro to gasp.

"Madre de Dios."

The odor Alejandro had smelled was blood. Tanner's face and clothing had been speckled, splattered, and stained by the blood of twenty-two men. Alejandro was the last member of his gang alive. The rest had died either while asleep or after having awakened in intense, but brief, pain.

Armstrong had killed an innocent child to send a message. Tanner would write him a reply in the blood of the guilty.

Tanner pressed the gun against the bridge of Alejandro's chilled nose. "Since you're the only one with a heater in his room I'm thinking that makes you the boss. Where can I find Armstrong and Lennox?"

Alejandro's eyes crossed comically for a second as his pupils stared at the gun. He then called out to his men in a loud voice.

"Santiago! Manuel! Emiliano! Sebastian! Hey! Answer me."

"They can't hear you; they're dead."

"Dead? All of them?"

"All of them."

Alejandro absorbed that news as his eyes darted around. "How many of you are there?"

"I killed them all one by one. I saved you for last because of the heater. If any of them made noise, you were unlikely to hear it. None of them made much noise, and they'll never make a sound again."

"Who... who the fuck are you?"

"My name is Tanner. Where do I find Armstrong and Lennox?"

"I don't know Lennox, but Armstrong is coming here later."

"That's a lie; I overheard your men talking. Armstrong won't be here for days."

"He'll still be here. And if he doesn't see me when he shows up, he'll know something's wrong."

"I can't wait days," Tanner said.

ARMSTRONG WAS STANDING OUT ON A SMALL TERRACE drinking yet another cup of coffee. He'd been up all night. Although chilly, the noon sun was warming him, and the hot coffee helped.

The men he had hired were on their way and expected soon. Three of them had a side trip to see to first. If Tanner appeared, Armstrong would be ready for him. He'd also sent two of his own people to the Eighth Street bar. They'd found the bodies of Benny, Gary, and Griffey.

When hours went by with nothing else happening, Armstrong figured that the man killing his people had gotten the message and was standing down, afraid that Armstrong would murder Makayla.

He hadn't wanted to kill the other girl. After all, she had been worth money to him, but he needed to make a point.

"Holy shit!"

That exclamation had come from Gramps. He was sitting in the living room and watching a game show when the news came on.

Armstrong slid open a glass door and called to him. "What's up?"

"I... they're... you've got to come see this for yourself."

Armstrong entered the room and moved to where he could see the TV. On the screen was an aerial view of a small lake. In the distance there appeared to be a shoreline. Something had been assembled by the edge of the lake. Logs? No, not logs. It took a moment for Armstrong to understand what he was looking at. The truth struck him at the same time the news anchor explained it.

"As we warned, these are graphic images. Those are bodies, ladies and gentlemen, twenty-three in all. They were arranged to spell out a name, the name—"

"Makayla," Armstrong said. "That spells Makayla."

Tanner's message had been delivered.

MY NAME IS TANNER

BECAUSE MAKAYLA'S NAME WAS UNCOMMON AND already in the news, it didn't go unnoticed that the dead Columbians spelled out the name of a recently abducted teen.

One commentator who was a former police officer speculated that the men were killed by a rival gang. He also said with some authority that it would have taken a dozen men or more to have killed Alejandro and his men. Crime scene evidence and forensics would prove that assertion false in the coming days.

Gramps was pointing at the TV screen. "That's the lodge where Alejandro and his boys are. Those bodies are theirs. Good God, Armstrong, who the fuck did that kid sic on us?"

Armstrong fell into a chair. "I'll ask him that when I see him."

"The kid?"

Armstrong ran a hand over his face. "I told some of the men I hired to grab the kid. I need to know what we're dealing with."

Gramps looked back at the screen where he had paused the image of the bodies. "We're dealing with death, that's what we're dealing with. That kid must have summoned a damn demon. Look at that. Imagine doing that. Forget killing them, that was the easy part. The son of a bitch then had to drag or carry each one of those men away from the lodge and place them like that. How long do you think that took, how much effort? He was sending you a message, give him the girl or die."

Armstrong wanted to respond with a denial but knew Gramps spoke the truth. Whoever had wiped out the Columbians was issuing a warning. He had killed a girl to try to make the man back off. Instead, the guy raised the stakes on him. Armstrong rose from his chair and headed outside. He no longer felt the sun, only the chill.

His destination was the garage where the girls were being held. It was a large structure that could hold up to four vehicles. The man who'd built the house had been a mechanic and liked to restore antique cars in his spare time. The garage had been designed with that in mind. It had a bathroom with a sink that the mechanic had used to wash up after a repair job was completed. The concrete floor was dotted by grease and oil stains.

The home's new owner used the space for a different purpose, as a holding pen for abducted girls and women. Parked in front of the garage was the motor home that Gramps drove.

The old woman was in the garage. She looked up in surprise when Armstrong entered. Other than an initial viewing of them to judge how much they were worth on the open market, Armstrong never gave the girls a second look.

When he asked her for one of the teens the night before she figured he was going to use one for sex. It shocked her to learn that he had killed the girl as a way to send a message. It also made her angry. Each of the girls were worth money to her. Once sold, she would be paid a percentage. No one paid a dime for a dead girl. Armstrong frowned when he noticed that she was passing sandwiches through the bars of the cages.

"They were all behaving, so I gave them some food."

Ellie was there too. Unlike the others she wasn't kept in a cage. Instead, she had a spot in the corner of the garage. In place of a mattress, she was given a large dog bed to sleep on. The little girl walked over to Armstrong and took his hand.

"Granny gave me some candy with my bologna sandwich because I was extra good the other day."

Armstrong patted her on the head like a pet. Using the motor home to transport the girls had been Griffey's brainchild, but Ellie was Armstrong's idea.

Years earlier one of the men had carjacked a woman to abduct her. The fool had never noticed the sleeping toddler in the car seat behind him. Armstrong had killed the man for his stupidity, sold the twenty-year-old victim, and kept her two-year-old child, Ellie. One look at her and he knew she would make excellent bait. Not many women would blindly follow a strange guy to a van, but they would trust a child who appeared to be in distress.

Best of all, Ellie worked for the price of a little food. When a few more years passed and she went through puberty, Armstrong would sell her and make a nice profit. By then, he'd have to snatch another girl to train and take Ellie's place. No problem. Children went missing all the time.

Armstrong told Ellie to leave the garage with Granny as he walked over to the cage that contained Makayla. He was staring down at her as if he wanted to kill her.

"There's a man causing me trouble. What's his name?"

"I... what man? I don't know what you mean."

"That damn boyfriend of yours asked for help during a press conference. Whoever is helping him has gone too far."

Makayla lit up in a smile. "Henry is alive?"

"He won't be for long, bitch. I'm going to find out who this friend of his is and then I'm going to kill all of you if I have to."

Makayla began crying. "My grandfather will pay you to leave us alone." She gestured toward the other cages. "He'll pay for all of us."

"Maybe, but I'd have one hell of a time getting the money without winding up in a cell."

Makayla bit her bottom lip. "He would still pay."

Armstrong stared down at her. The girl knew nothing. He'd have to wait until he had Henry to get answers.

He had left the garage and was walking back to the house when his phone rang. Looking down at the screen he saw that he had a call from a dead man, Benny. He cursed himself for not already getting rid of the phone. The cops could have come across the bodies in the bar and were trying to make contact with the last person to speak to Benny. Armstrong was about to destroy his phone when he realized it could be someone else calling. It could be the man who was causing him nothing but grief. He answered the phone on the eleventh ring.

"Yeah?"

"Is this Armstrong?"

"Who's this?"

"I'm the man looking for Makayla. My name is Tanner. If that name means anything to you then you know that I won't stop until I've found you. Let Makayla go and I'll let you live."

"Tanner? You're a damn hit man? That punk ass kid is friends with a hit man?"

"You killed a girl to send me a message. By now, I'm guessing you've seen my reply. That will tell you how serious I am."

"Yeah, you killed Alejandro and his gang, but I have other buyers for the girls."

"You heard me, Armstrong. Let Makayla go free or die. Either way, I will find you. If Makayla is free, you'll live."

"Tanner."

"Yeah?"

"You've fucked with the wrong man."

"There is no Mr. Lennox, is there? You're Mr. Lennox."

Armstrong hung up without responding. He stood out in front of the house with his mind racing.

Tanner, Goddamn Tanner.

Armstrong recalled the stories he'd heard about

the man. He had thought they were bullshit. They weren't bullshit. Tanner had wiped out Alejandro and his men and laid them out in the sun like they were stalks left to dry.

Tanner claimed he'd let him live if he gave up the girl. Armstrong doubted that was true. There was only one way out, and that was to kill Tanner before he could reach him. The man had chewed through his other people like a hungry shark. There was no reason to believe he wouldn't find his way to them.

Armstrong ran a hand over his scalp and felt the rough surface, as he had yet to shave. The cold was ignored as he paced in front of the house. When a plan came to him, he stood still and thought it over. He figured it had a good chance of working and that Tanner would walk into a trap.

He rushed into the house and told Gramps and Granny that they were leaving. The two of them were in the kitchen talking. Ellie sat in a corner of the room drawing on a pad.

"I thought it was too risky to move the girls?" Gramps said.

"It would be even riskier to stay. Get those bitches loaded onto the RV. I want to be out of here in less than an hour."

"What about the guys who are coming here?"

"They should be here any minute. They'll be

staying. When Tanner shows up, they'll be ready to greet him."

"Who's Tanner?"

"That's who killed Alejandro and the others, Tanner."

"Tanner? You mean *Tanner*, Tanner? The hitter?"

"That's him."

"Holy shit. No wonder Alejandro and his boys are dead. We've got to get out of here, Armstrong. Tanner might know where we are."

"The faster you get those girls on the motor home the sooner we get out of here. And another thing, wipe this place down good. We don't need the cops finding our prints."

Gramps rose from the table, along with Granny. When the old woman told Ellie to follow her, Armstrong said no.

"Ellie is staying here. I have a special job for her."

The old couple left the room. Ellie got up from the floor and walked over to Armstrong. The hideous truth being that he was the closest thing to a father figure she had.

"What do you want me to do?"

Armstrong smiled. "I need you to be sneaky."

"Like when I trick the girls?"

"No, even sneakier. You're going to be my secret weapon."

14

SURPRISE ATTACK

Henry had seen the news report about Alejandro and his men. A short time later, a reporter tweeted that an anonymous source stated that the dead men were drug runners and suspected of being connected to an investigation into white slavery. Numerous weapons had been recovered from the scene along with drugs.

When Henry saw that the corpses had been used to spell out Makayla's name, he knew it was Tanner's handiwork. Agent X was kicking ass and taking names.

His grandmother had been aghast by the scene. "My God. Twenty-three men. There must have been a gang war. But why would a rival gang spell out Makayla's name like that?"

"It must be about a different Makayla," Henry said.

"Is that likely? Makayla is a fairly rare name."

Henry said nothing more. He didn't think Tanner wanted his grandmother to know what was going on. And yet, she was no fool. As she said, Henry asked for help and Cody appeared. Still, she wasn't going to believe that one man could have killed twenty-three by himself. But Cody wasn't just any man, he was a Tanner, a living legend.

When Henry hadn't responded to her, Laura sighed. "Are you still angry with me?"

Henry was perturbed by his grandmother's refusal to tell him more about his father. Whoever the man was, he was wanted by the law.

They were in the kitchen preparing to eat lunch. Laura was cooking burgers and fries atop the stove. Although it was a school day, Henry was off. There was no way he could concentrate on schoolwork while Makayla was missing.

A commercial break ended, and the 24-hour news station came back on. On screen was the photo of a beautiful blonde girl about Henry's age. Beneath her picture was her name.

"This just in, fingerprints found at the scene of that massacre near Lake Erie were those of sixteen-year-old Candace Harper. The teen went missing while walking home from a friend's house in

Virginia in September. This seems to indicate that she had been held by the gang for a time."

"Oh no," Laura said. "Those men could have had Makayla too."

Henry, who had always had phenomenal hearing, heard the sound of whispered voices coming from outside the windows in the kitchen. He was up out of his seat and going for his rifle when the back door was kicked in.

Three men came through the door with guns in their hands. Henry had left his rifle leaning against the side of the refrigerator. While he was grabbing it, he was out of sight of the men, the first of whom grabbed a screaming Laura by her shoulders and yanked her away from the stove.

"Where's the boy?" one of the other men asked.

Henry answered his question by firing three rounds at the man. The slugs ripped open the mercenary's chest and he fell back against the third man, nearly knocking him down. That man recovered and shoved the dying form of his companion at Henry. Henry was able to get off one more shot before the body collided into him. The round struck the third guy in the head, killing him.

Unfortunately for Henry, the weight of the body thrown against him caused him to fall backwards, and as he fell, he struck his skull hard against the edge of a counter. Henry tumbled to the floor with one of his victims landing on top of him.

"Henry!" Laura cried out. The man holding her was looking around in shock. Three armed and experienced men had been sent to abduct a boy and a middle-aged woman. Within seconds of entering the house without warning, two of them were dead.

He cuffed Laura and pushed her to the floor. "Stay down there or I'll shoot your ass."

The man rushed over to Henry, claimed the rifle, and pushed his dying associate off the boy he'd been ordered to bring back.

"Don't be dead, kid," the man said as he checked Henry's limp form for a pulse.

"Is he all right?" Laura asked.

"His pulse is steady, but he'll have a good knot on the back of his head." The mercenary used the leather strap on the M1 to sling it on his back. Afterward, he bent down, adjusted Henry's weight onto his shoulder, and stood.

"Get up, woman. And if you give me any trouble, I swear I'll drop you where you stand. I need the boy, but I was told you were expendable."

"Who sent you here?"

The guy pointed the gun at her face. He had a full beard; above it was a pair of cold eyes. "Just keep your mouth shut and do what I tell you."

Laura said nothing more. She could tell the man

was making a promise and not a threat. His eyes flicked down to take in the dead forms of his friends and he gritted his teeth in anger. After leaving the house, the man trudged along with Henry on his shoulder while keeping Laura in front of him.

As they reached the end of the driveway Laura saw a black van with its side door sitting open. Her abductor ordered her to get inside. Laura did so and sat on a floor that was covered in thick plastic. The man lowered Henry beside her. Before getting behind the wheel he bound Laura's ankles, gagged her, then bound Henry's wrists and ankles, and slapped tape over his mouth.

As they drove away, back at the house, the kitchen began filling with smoke. The food Laura had been cooking was burning. Within minutes a grease fire would start, and the house would be aflame. Two bodies lay inside the structure, and there were two residents of the home. It would initially be reported that the dead were believed to be Henry and his grandmother.

Tanner would have no knowledge of that sad news. By then, he would have trouble of his own.

15

A WELL-LAID TRAP

ARMSTRONG ABANDONED THE HOUSE WHERE HE'D been holding the girls and moved to another location. He left behind the mercenaries he'd hired. Armstrong didn't know how the hit man would do so, but he expected Tanner to find the house. When he did, hired killers would be waiting for him.

The man leading the dozen mercenaries Armstrong employed was named Dutch. Dutch had heard of Tanner and had respect for his abilities. In fact, he had made it a point to discover as much about him as he could over the years. By doing so, he had learned that Tanner was fond of using diversion and doing the unexpected. In Dutch's opinion, it was why the hit man was a formidable opponent.

He relayed this to the man who was second-in-charge, McCawley, along with the other seven men who were with him. Three others had been sent to grab Henry. Dutch had yet to learn of the difficulty they'd had.

While Dutch looked every bit the soldier, a big man with a steely gaze, McCawley was deceptively timid-looking. Although he stood nearly six feet tall, McCawley was thin, wore glasses, and had sallow, freckled skin that made him look as if he'd spent his life indoors.

Appearance aside, McCawley was deadly with a knife and fast and accurate with a gun. Dutch had accepted the assignment and was glad he had McCawley along when he discovered their target was Tanner.

"I heard Tanner was tricky, but do you know what's meant by that?" McCawley asked.

"Oh yeah," Dutch said. "Did any of you guys ever hear how he took out Alonso Alvarado down in Mexico?"

No one had, so Dutch relayed the tale to them.

"I was in that area of Mexico a couple of years ago and heard the story from one of the cartel members who took over after Alvarado was dead. Tanner had joined up with a guy and a woman, then they wore disguises to make themselves look like someone else. Not just anyone else, but people they knew Alvarado wanted to kidnap. It worked. Alvarado sent men to grab them and they were brought into the compound. That's how Tanner got past the hundreds of men Alvarado had guarding him. He tricked the bastard into waltzing him right on in by pretending to be someone else. Hundreds of armed men and Tanner let himself be taken without having a weapon on him."

"That was ballsy," said one of the other men.

"Yeah, and clever as hell," Dutch said. "When Tanner gets here, he won't be coming at us head on. We need to be prepared for a diversion or some sort of distraction. Whatever it is, if it happens in front of us, expect Tanner to come from behind. If there's trouble on your left, look to your right."

"We'll still need to investigate anything that happens," McCawley said.

"And we will, you and I," Dutch said. "But the rest of these guys will stay back and be ready for an attack from a different direction. We're prepared for Tanner. We've got motion detectors and cameras set up so he can't get near us without letting us know. Just remember, if it looks like he's coming at us from one way, it's more likely a trick and he's approaching from another direction."

Most of the men were in their late twenties and early thirties. The youngest man was nineteen. He was named Devon. He smiled and pumped a fist in the air.

"When we nail this bastard, we'll all be famous. Everyone thinks Tanner is such hot shit."

Dutch pointed a warning finger at him. "He's everything they say he is, so don't get cocky, Devon."

"I'm cool, and I won't fall for any of his tricks."

"All right then, let's get into position and we'll see what Tanner throws at us."

ARMSTRONG HAD BEEN RIGHT ABOUT TANNER tracking down the location of the house.

Tanner did so by working from an assumption. The home where Henry had been found and the home where Trigger held women were similar types. They were both set in secluded areas and their garages were unattached.

Thanks to Benny, Tanner had the name of the town, he just needed an address. Despite there being over a thousand homes, finding those that matched the criteria whittled the list down to only a few score. That many would still have taken Tanner a week to check out. However, that list was cut dramatically when Tanner considered one more known fact.

Armstrong had Gramps and Granny transport the girls inside an RV. Not many people owned such a vehicle. Of those who did in the town, only four of them owned homes with land and a detached garage.

Tanner had gone online and used a popular mapping service to look at the town from an overhead view. It had taken quite awhile but he had found the four homes that matched what he had been looking for. Each one had a large vehicle parked outside that appeared to be a motor home. It was possible that there were other homes with RVs that had the vehicles out of the driveway on the day the mapping was performed. If so, and if Armstrong's property was one of them, then Tanner was out of luck and would have to find another way to locate him. He had decided to scout the four homes out and see if his idea worked. The first two houses were discarded as possibilities right away.

There had been people about. One was a mother with two young children and a man in a wheelchair. The other had been a retired couple. Tanner had considered they might be Gramps and Granny, but then an SUV arrived, and a woman got out of it. She addressed the old couple as Mom and Dad and gave them hugs, so Tanner moved on to check out the other two houses on the list.

He never needed to visit the fourth home. Number three on the list was the one he'd been looking for. He knew that after climbing a tree with a pair of binoculars and seeing armed men walking around. He'd also spotted the men installing cameras and motion detectors at the direction of a big man who was obviously their leader. Tanner had often used cameras and motion detectors himself; they were an effective way to cover a large area.

What Tanner hadn't seen was an RV. That meant the girls were gone and he could be walking into a trap. It didn't matter. The house was simply another link in the chain. It would get him one step closer to finding Makayla.

After climbing down from the tree, Tanner went back to his Jeep. He had retrieved the vehicle after leaving the bar in Altoona. He'd also made a second stop in order to acquire things he needed to cause a distraction. After going over the plan in his mind, Tanner readied himself for an assault. This included eating something to provide energy. He'd gone without sleep for over twenty-four hours and had been active.

Gramps had been accurate when he said that arranging the Columbians' dead bodies took great effort. It had, but it was also worth it. Tanner had been sending Armstrong a message. He'd been letting him know what he was up against.

He hadn't expected Armstrong to give in and agree to release Makayla. He had hoped that it would keep the man from killing the girl. Armstrong knew that Tanner wouldn't quit. If he were to murder Makayla, the man would know that there would be nowhere to hide that Tanner wouldn't find him.

No, a guy like Armstrong would want to take at least one more shot at killing Tanner before he considered giving in. He would live in hope of coming out on top.

And if Tanner survived and eventually reached him, Armstrong would want to have Makayla nearby as a hostage or to use her to bargain for his life. Either way, the deaths of the Columbians had bought Makayla more time. It was time that Tanner hoped to put to good use.

DUTCH AND MCCAWLEY HAD BEEN TALKING ABOUT what to do if Tanner didn't show before nighttime. That was when a beep from his phone told Dutch that someone had tripped one of the motion detectors on the east side of the property.

He and his men were in contact with each other via hands-free communication devices. He let them know that something was happening.

"There's movement to our east. McCawley and I will check it out. The rest of you keep aware and pay attention to the west. This could be one of Tanner's tricks."

The others answered that they understood and Dutch left cover and headed east along the property's hurricane fence. McCawley followed close behind Dutch while watching their flanks. It wasn't long before they came upon a board in the fence that had been loosened. The board was wide enough to allow someone to slip inside. Dutch pointed it out to McCawley, who nodded.

"Do you think Tanner came in that—" McCawley stopped speaking as a voice came over his earpiece. At the same time, Dutch's phone beeped again.

"There's movement west, Dutch."

Dutch looked down at his phone's screen and saw that a motion detector at the other side of the property had been set off. That was where the gate was.

"Move in and take the target down. Kill him if you have to. McCawley and I are on the way."

"You called it, Dutch," said a grinning McCawley.

"Yeah, if you're sneaky long enough you become predictable. Let's go get this fucker."

They were nearing the gate when the shouting began. His men were telling someone to drop their weapon. That person must have ignored the warning, because a barrage of shots soon followed. The sounds were muffled, as his men's rifles were equipped with silencers. Still, the shots were distinct in the calm of a winter day in the country.

They were quiet enough to do what they were meant to do, keep the neighbors from hearing and responding to the sound of gunfire. Armstrong wanted to be able to return to the property if possible once the threat was eliminated. He also said there would be a bonus for Dutch and his people if they managed to kill Tanner without attracting attention.

As Dutch grew near to his men, he saw that they were clustered around a body. The man on the ground was wounded and dying. He'd been shot six times in the torso along with other wounds to his extremities. After moaning, the figure exhaled and lay still. It was the stillness of the newly dead.

Devon had been attempting to kick the gun out of the man's hand, but the guy had a literal death grip on it. He gave up and tried pulling off his mask instead. That too resisted being removed.

"I think it's glued on," Devon said. "And shit, the gun is glued to his hand. No wonder the fucker didn't drop it when we told him to. Why the hell would he glue it to his hand?"

Another of the men had been checking a cloth ammo pouch that was attached to the dead man's belt.

"There's nothing in here but nails, and I think I see a phone."

"Nails and a phone?" McCawley said, his face

screwed up in confusion. When he looked over at Dutch, he saw the look of alarm in his friend's eyes.

"Down, down, everybody down!" Dutch shouted. He said the words while diving away from the body and covering his head with his arms. At that same moment the phone inside the ammo pouch went off. It was one of the flash-bang grenades Tanner had gotten from Duke. The blast was a fraction of what a real grenade would be, but it was enough to propel the nails and turn them into mini missiles. They tore through Dutch's men and caused numerous wounds.

McCawley lost an eye while most of the others suffered more than a dozen painful, though not serious injuries to their abdomens and legs. Only Dutch avoided the pain of the nails, as he was prone on the ground. Several of the nails had struck the bottom of his boots and one protruded from the side of his heel.

The dead man with the mask and gun glued on was Trigger. Tanner had freed him from his cage when he realized he could be put to better use as a decoy. He then made him march on ahead of him toward the house. The ski mask and the gun were glued to him. Tanner had also glued his lips together so that he couldn't talk.

Upon Tanner's return to the garage, Trigger begged to be released from the cage. He hadn't liked living in the cage as he had made so many others do.

He had gotten his wish and was set free, only to die as a pawn.

Dutch had made it up to his knees when Tanner began blasting away with a shotgun. He assumed that he would be outnumbered and knew that the effects of the stun grenade would only provide a temporary advantage. By using a shotgun, he was able to take down more than one man at a time.

Dutch spun on his knees and raised his rifle. He didn't have a shot. McCawley and the others were blocking his view of Tanner.

He dropped to the ground again to take aim at Tanner's lower limbs, which he could see. Before he could fire, Tanner leapt up and placed a scissor lock on McCawley's neck. When Tanner fell to the ground with McCawley, he twisted his body so that it sent McCawley spinning toward Dutch.

Dutch grunted in pain as his friend fell atop him. McCawley's weight had dislocated Dutch's left shoulder and stunned him. By the time Dutch recovered, Tanner had made it to his feet, having claimed Dutch's rifle from his hands. The hit man fired the gun in three-round bursts to kill the rest of his men. Dutch freed himself from McCawley's weight and tried to run away, his movements were off-balance because of the nails stuck in the soles of his boots. He was cut down as a round caught him in the back of the leg. After shooting McCawley in the head, Tanner approached Dutch. He was masked as Trigger had been because he had spotted the security cameras as he did his reconnaissance.

Dutch turned over and looked up into Tanner's intense eyes. "Let me live and I'll tell you where Armstrong is."

"You'll tell me either way," Tanner said. As he was speaking, he freed a knife.

DUTCH HELD OUT FOR OVER A MINUTE BEFORE telling Tanner what he needed to know. He died last and in great pain.

Tanner entered the garage after using a rock to shatter one of the structure's blacked-out windows. Although he didn't expect to find Makayla and the other abducted girls inside, he still felt the disappointment when he saw that they weren't there.

He nearly missed the small figure huddled in a corner of the garage. It was Ellie, she had been lying in the middle of her dog bed.

The little girl was shivering from fright as Tanner climbed through the window and approached her. She had heard Dutch's screams of agony.

"Please don't hurt me, mister."

"I won't hurt you," Tanner said. He rolled up the

mask so that Ellie could see his face. There were no cameras inside the garage. "Is anyone else around?"

"Mr. Armstrong left along with Gramps and Granny. He told me to stay here and wait for him."

"What's your name?"

"Ellie."

Tanner gestured at the bed. "Is there a dog here?"

"It's my bed."

Tanner sighed with disgust at the way Armstrong had treated the child. He offered her a hand to help her stand up. Ellie took it, then embraced Tanner in a hug.

"Can I get some food? I'm hungry."

"You'll be taken care of. I'm sure there are cops on the way. Stay here and they'll find you, okay?"

Ellie didn't answer. She was concentrating on doing the task Armstrong had given her. She had a hypodermic needle hidden down the left sleeve of her jacket, one she freed with her right hand. It was filled with the same sedative Sal and Vernon had used to drug Makayla during her abduction. Tanner felt the movement as Ellie tugged the cap off. Looking back over his shoulder he saw her small hand bringing the needle toward him.

Tanner pushed her away, but not before the needle slipped under the hem of his jacket, pierced the material of his shirt, and broke his skin. Ellie had managed to jab him and inject at least some of the drug into his system. The needle had stabbed and scraped the flesh of his lower back.

"What the hell, kid?"

Ellie came at him again. Tanner used his foot to shove her backwards. Ellie tripped over her own feet and fell onto her bottom. It was when she was attempting to get up that she saw the needle sticking out of her hand.

"Uh-oh," she said, as she pulled the needle free. Ellie's eyes fluttered, drooped, fluttered again, then closed as she lowered herself the rest of the way to the floor. Despite her treachery, Tanner was relieved to see that her chest was moving. Had she taken in a greater dose of the drug it might have killed her. She was more of a pawn than Trigger had been, and every bit the innocent.

Tanner felt his own eyes growing heavy, as the drug had an effect on him. When he began moving toward the door, it was an effort to stay on his feet. By the time he reached the window the sound of police sirens was in the air and growing closer. Tanner had left the Jeep parked on a knoll among trees; it was nearly a mile away. The way he was feeling, he'd be lucky to climb back out the window without falling onto his face. He wasn't going to get away before the police arrived. He needed a place to hide.

There were limited choices and time was

running out, as it was becoming a struggle to stay awake. Ellie had injected but a small portion of the sedative into him, but it had been enough. The lack of sleep he'd experienced only heightened its effectiveness.

There was an old truck in the garage that had all four tires going flat. It had been sitting there for a long time. All it had going for it was that it was better than nothing. Tanner lowered himself to the oil-stained floor and began crawling beneath the old junker. Lying prone was seductive and all he wanted was to close his eyes and go to sleep.

As his hand touched something rough, he explored it further and came upon a surprise, a very pleasant one. Within seconds, he was beneath the truck and unable to remain awake. Two officers entered the garage minutes later, as more arrived on the scene. The neighbors, although some distance away, had reported hearing the explosion, the roar of the shotgun, and Dutch's screams of pain.

Tanner never heard the cops enter. Ellie had done her job well. Tanner was out cold, and at the mercy of anyone who found him.

16

A REASON TO CELEBRATE

ARMSTRONG WAS STARING AT HENRY WITH A CURIOUS gaze after learning the boy had killed two of the three men sent to grab him. Henry had recovered from the blow to the back of his skull while in the van. His head hurt but there was no dizziness.

Seeing his grandmother tied up and gagged filled him with a sense of disgust. He had once again failed to protect someone he loved. As he recalled the moments before he blacked out, he was certain he had killed two men. That knowledge neither sickened him nor thrilled him. Those men had broken into their home to do them harm and he had responded as needed. Maybe if he'd been a little older or had some training, he could have defeated all three of them. If he had been like Tanner, the men wouldn't have stood a chance against him.

They had been on the road for nearly an hour when the van made a turn onto a road bordered by leafless oak trees. From where he lay, Henry had a view out the top of the windshield. The sound of tires rolling over gravel came after the next turn, as they entered the long winding driveway of an isolated house.

The van stopped and the driver got out. That was followed by voices that were too far away for Henry to make out what they were saying, even with his exceptional hearing. Moments later, the side door on the van slid open and Henry saw a black man with a shaved head staring at him. It was Armstrong, and he was holding Henry's rifle.

"You've caused me a lot of trouble, boy."

Henry attempted to speak, but the tape covering his mouth muffled his words. Armstrong told the mercenary to take Laura away.

"Put her with the girls inside the barn; there's an empty cage."

Laura's ankles were freed so she could walk, then she was yanked out of the van and pulled along by her arm. She gazed back at Henry for as long as she could.

Armstrong reached inside the van and tore the tape from Henry's lips.

After moving his tongue around, Henry spoke.

"You're the guy who killed those other men when Makayla was taken. I recognize your voice."

"That's right, and I'll kill your grandmother if you give me any more grief."

"Why did you kidnap us?"

"You're my insurance against Tanner."

Henry was unable to conceal the surprise he felt at learning that Armstrong knew Tanner's name.

Armstrong smiled. "That's right. I know it was Tanner you begged to help you during that press conference. What I want to know is how a punk teenager knows the man well enough that he would help you... are you related to him?"

"We're not related. I met him when I was ten and he killed the man who murdered my mother. He helped me then and he's helping me now."

"Wrong. Tanner will be dead soon, if he's not already. I set a trap for him that he won't see coming."

Henry laughed, causing Armstrong to glare at him.

"What's so funny?"

"Tanner is Tanner, and you, you're a guy who picks on girls to make money. Tanner will survive whatever trap you've set up and come here to kill you."

Armstrong raised Henry's rifle and aimed it at

the boy's face. Henry met his gaze without blinking. If he was afraid of the gun, he hid it well.

Armstrong lowered the rifle. "You've got balls, boy, I'll give you that."

"What's your name?"

"Why would I tell you that?"

"Why not? I've already seen your face; that means you're planning to kill me, right?"

"Yeah, that's right. Call me Armstrong."

"Hey, Armstrong?"

"What?"

"You'll be dead by this time tomorrow unless you let us all go. If you do that, I'll tell Tanner to let you live."

"I'll take my chances," Armstrong said. Afterward, he turned away from Henry and yelled to two of his people. He had called in the troops, so to speak, by having the rest of his people come to his new location. It was where he would make a stand if Tanner survived Dutch and his men. Even if that happened, Tanner might still be taken unawares by Ellie. He had given the little girl a syringe with enough sedative to kill Tanner, and a child would be the last one Tanner would suspect of treachery.

When his men came over, he told them to lock Henry up in an old planting shed that was on the property.

"Let me see Makayla," Henry said.

"Worry about your own ass, boy. Take him away."

As Henry was dragged off, Armstrong took out his phone and called Dutch. There was no answer. The fact that there was no answer made a tiny pit of fear bloom in Armstrong's gut. It had been so long since he'd felt the emotion that he almost didn't recognize it.

If Dutch wasn't answering his phone that could mean he was dead. If he was dead, it was Tanner that killed him. Dutch knew where Armstrong had moved to; he had needed to know so he could tell his men where to bring Henry and his grandmother. Armstrong took in a deep breath and released it slowly. There was no need to worry until he knew more.

The new house was smaller than the others but was surrounded by more land. It had been a farmhouse years earlier, until the farmer and his two sons died in a traffic accident. Armstrong had bought the property cheap after the farmer's widow had lost it to a bank foreclosure.

Gramps and Granny shared the guest room while Armstrong took the master bedroom. His men had to make do in the home's finished basement. There were foldout couches down there and an electric fireplace for heat.

Along with the mercenary who'd brought Henry to the home he had six men and Gramps and

Granny. If Tanner wasn't dead, Armstrong might be forced to admit defeat, leave the girls, and head out of the state to avoid Tanner. Tanner would not be stopped by six men and a couple of senior citizens. If Armstrong left Makayla alive and made an anonymous call to the cops, maybe Tanner would stop looking for him. Yeah, maybe.

As usual, Gramps was watching TV, another damn game show. Armstrong told him to see if he could find a local news channel. As Gramps was flipping through the channels, a familiar sight came on the screen. It was a scene of the front gate at the property they had abandoned only hours earlier. An off-screen reporter was saying that a gun battle had taken place there.

"Damn it!" Armstrong said. "I was hoping that place wouldn't get burned. Not only did it cost me a down payment but now I can no longer use the identity I bought it under."

Gramps pointed at the TV. "Look at the words scrolling along the bottom of the screen. It says there are ten dead, but you only left nine guys there. Shit. Do you think Tanner killed Ellie too?"

Before Armstrong could answer, clarification came as the reporter appeared on screen near an ambulance.

"As we said earlier, there were ten dead men discovered at the scene along with a young girl. The girl was found unconscious but is expected to recover fully. I'm told that one of the dead men was wearing a mask. Police are still struggling to piece together what went on here."

The reporter signed off as a huge smile appeared on Armstrong's face.

"Yes! The man wearing a mask must be Tanner. He killed Dutch and his men and came across Ellie. That little girl must have done what a hundred men couldn't do, she killed Tanner."

Gramps was scratching his head. "How could Ellie kill Tanner? Don't tell me you gave her a gun."

Armstrong explained about the syringe and the drug. Gramps was laughing by the time he finished.

"That was genius. Tanner never saw Ellie coming. It's too bad we can't get her back, but she's in the hands of the cops now."

"I'll have someone grab another child. No, better yet, two of them. After a few years of training they'll be like Ellie."

"Now that Tanner is dead, what are you going to do with the kid and his grandmother?"

"I'll find a buyer for both of them. It will help to make up for the grief and the expense that little bastard caused me."

"You shouldn't have much trouble selling that boy, but I don't know about his grandmother. She's a good-looking woman but she ain't young."

"There are whorehouses in Mexico that will take her. Or maybe I'll shoot her in front of the kid to give him some grief. I don't really care. I'm just glad that Tanner is dead. In a week or two, things will get back to normal."

Gramps laughed. "Little Ellie killed Tanner. Son of a bitch."

"Wrong. *I* killed Tanner; Ellie was only the weapon I used."

"This will make you a big man to a lot of people, but you should stay out of New York City. I hear Joe Pullo and Tanner were friends."

"It's not something I plan to brag about. I don't need the grief a man like Pullo could give me." Armstrong slapped his hands together and started toward the kitchen. "I'm going to get something to eat; my appetite is back."

"Have a bologna sandwich, in honor of Ellie."

Armstrong laughed. "Hell, I just might do that."

17

THE PIT

Eight hours after Tanner had his firefight with Dutch and his men, Sara stared at her phone in frustration. She was seated in the living room at her father's house in Connecticut and had been unable to get ahold of Tanner. She was concerned but not worried. If there was anyone who could take care of themselves, it was Tanner.

Sara was more worried about Henry. She had learned of the blaze that consumed his home and for a short time believed the worst. The two men killed during Henry and his grandmother's abduction had been burned beyond recognition in the fire and were at first thought to be Henry and Laura.

That only lasted until the coroner arrived on the scene, then the news reported that they were the bodies of two unidentified adult males. Both men had been shot to death.

The relief Sara felt was marred by the knowledge that Henry was missing. She wondered if it had anything to do with the men who had taken Makayla Albertini.

Sara tried calling Tanner again. There was no answer. She put her phone down. He would call when he could. Like many, she had viewed the scene on the news of the twenty-three dead men who spelled out Makayla's name. No one needed to tell her that it had been Tanner's handiwork. He was on the hunt for the men who had Makayla. There was nothing and no one who could stop him from finding her.

Warren Blake, Sara's father, entered the room and handed her a cup of coffee. Before sitting down, Warren peeked at his grandson. Lucas was sleeping on the sofa beside Sara after having played for hours with his cousin, Emily.

"Did you reach your husband yet?"

"No, but he'll call when he can."

"Do you really think he'll find that girl?"

"Cody will find her. He does whatever he puts his mind to."

Warren shook his head in dismay. "When I learned that you were marrying a criminal, and a hit man no less, I thought you had lost your mind. But I have to admit he's a hell of a man."

"He admires you too. Now, what's this I hear about you having a girlfriend?"

"I see your sister has been talking."

"So, it's true?"

"I'm seeing someone, yes. Her name is Nina. We met when she rented one of the properties I own."

"What is she like?"

"She's lovely, inside and out. I think you'll like her."

"Invite her over while I'm here so I can meet her."

"I wish I could, but Nina is on a buying trip right now for her chain of boutiques. But this is just a short visit. I want you and Cody to return soon and stay for a week, maybe around Easter."

"Are things serious between you and Nina?"

Warren hesitated, then nodded. "We've only been dating for a few weeks, but I know I want to see more of her. And there's something else too."

"What's that?"

"I've got a big murder case coming up... I'll be defending Zander Hall."

"The man accused of killing his wife and her lover? Oh Daddy, you've picked some client. You'll have a hard time finding a juror who likes him."

"Yes. He's not the most personable man I've ever met."

Sara laughed. "Personable? Zander Hall is a misogynist who makes no apologies about his opinions on women."

"Regardless of that, the man deserves a defense and I'm going to give it to him. I know the media coverage he's received so far makes him look guilty but there's no real evidence against him. In fact, there's evidence to suggest that Zander's wife and her lover killed each other. He also had three alibi witnesses that placed him elsewhere at the time the deaths took place."

"I heard he had them killed so that they couldn't change their stories."

Warren sighed. "Two died in accidents and the third went missing while on a hike. There's nothing to suggest my client was involved in any of that."

"I still think you have an uphill battle. Other than that, I'm glad you'll be back in the courtroom again. I know how much you love it."

"We'll see if it gets that far. I expect the DA to offer a plea deal. If it involves prison time my client won't sign off on it. When he hired me, all Hall wanted to know was if I could keep him out of prison."

"Can you?"

"I think so, given the evidence against him."

"I wish you luck."

Warren pointed over at Lucas. "When are you going to give me more grandchildren?"

"Someday. Cody and I both want more," Sara said. She looked down at her phone, wondering where he could be.

TANNER LAY IN DARKNESS AS HIS EYES FLUTTERED open. He had awoken once before, only to be dragged back down to sleep by the drug he'd been injected with. This time he fought to stay awake and managed to raise his head. He could see nothing, as all was darkness.

After running a hand over his face, he raised himself onto his hands and knees. The desire to lie back down was seductive, as he felt exhausted. It was then that he recalled where he was, and the peril he was in. That stirred him to greater wakefulness while also causing him to be careful in his movements, so as to make as little sound as possible.

The pit, I'm in the pit.

In desperation he had sought to be out of view by crawling beneath the old truck. The odds that he wouldn't be spotted there were slim but better than nothing. In fact, it had been the best move he could have possibly made.

The former owner of the property had been a car

mechanic who liked to work on vehicles even in his spare time. The large garage had been designed with that in mind. That included the installation of a mechanic's pit. It was essentially a hole in the floor that one could use to work on the undercarriage of a vehicle.

The trench had been beneath the old truck and was hidden by several sections of thick plywood that acted as a cover. The wood fit into grooves and appeared flush with the rest of the floor. As he crawled beneath the truck to hide, Tanner had felt the rough surface of the wood. When he realized there was empty space beneath the boards the thrill of discovering a refuge had given his system a boost. He was able to fight off the inexorable slide into unconsciousness brought on by the drug long enough to ease down into the pit. Tanner barely managed to slide the plywood back into its slot before he could no longer keep his eyes open and collapsed to the bottom of the hole, where he remained for many hours.

Tanner stood on unsteady legs and listened. He heard nothing. After easing out his phone he saw the time. He'd been out for nearly ten hours. He also saw the messages from Sara and knew she must be wondering why he hadn't responded. He would call her back and explain, but first he had to get out of the pit and away from the house.

He made as little noise as possible and still the rough edge of the plywood moving across the floor made a distinctive sound. When there was no response to the scraping of wood on concrete, Tanner figured there was no one in the garage and decided to move quicker.

Getting out of the pit took more energy than it should have. It reminded him that the drug wasn't out of his system. He would need to be cautious, careful, for he wasn't quite himself.

He slid the plywood back in place and used the side of the truck to help him stand. The metal was cold against his hand as the temperature was dropping overnight.

He moved toward the broken window he had used to enter the garage. The outside world was quiet. Overhead, clouds thickened as a storm predicted for the following day moved into the area.

The police had been and gone, and had removed the bodies of Dutch and his men. They had also taken away the child, Ellie. That was good. It meant she was out of Armstrong's reach and might be reunited with her family.

Tanner had to hand it to Armstrong. Using the girl against him had been a Machiavellian, if sick, move. If he had been a little less alert the girl might have given him a dose of the drug that would have killed him.

Climbing out of the window seemed like more trouble than it was worth given his diminished state. Tanner went to the door, found that the police had left it unlocked, and opened it to leave.

Mechanic's pit or not, had any of the dead been discovered inside the garage it would have become a crime scene. The police forensic techs would have gone over every inch of it and would have discovered him. Finding an unconscious Ellie didn't merit such action. It was the only reason he had remained undetected.

There was crime scene tape across the board Tanner had loosened on the east side of the property. He had to get down and crawl through the opening. Lying prone caused his eyelids to droop, as his body still craved sleep.

Once he was up on his feet again, Tanner paused to relieve his bladder. With that done, he quickened his pace in an effort to rouse himself. It helped, and when he reached the hill where he'd left the Jeep, the climb revived him more. And yet, he felt exhausted when he settled behind the wheel. Coffee, he needed strong coffee. But first, he had a call to make.

A SMILE AND A LOOK OF RELIEF LIT UP SARA'S FACE when she heard Tanner's voice.

"Are you all right?"

"I'm good, how are you and the baby?"

"We're great, but why were you out of reach for so long?"

Tanner went on to explain what had happened, including how he narrowly escaped capture.

"The little girl was mentioned on the news. They say she went missing along with her mother six years ago."

"Is she all right?"

"Yes, and the police contacted her family. But Cody, I have bad news."

Sara told him about the fire that gutted Henry's home and the two bodies found in the charred structure.

"It's not Henry and his grandmother," she added quickly. "The bodies belonged to two men who had yet to be identified... but Henry and Laura are missing."

"Armstrong must have them."

"Can you find him?"

"Yes, I think I know where he is. I also think he'll believe I was killed. He left nine men behind and the police recovered ten bodies. He'll believe Ellie killed me with that needle he gave her."

"Who was the tenth man?"

"A scumbag named Trigger. I used him as a diversion when I attacked."

"Let me help you. I can be back in the area by early morning."

"Henry might not have that long."

"But you're not at your peak; I can hear it in your voice."

"It's the drug, but it will wear off. Besides, Armstrong thinks I'm dead. He won't be expecting an attack."

"Please be careful."

"I'll be fine. Armstrong is all out of child assassins. Kiss Lucas for me, and I'll call you when I have Henry."

"I love you."

"I love you too, Sara."

Tanner started up the Jeep and drove out to the highway. After pulling into the drive-thru of a famous coffee franchise, he ordered two large cups of black coffee and three donuts. The caffeine and sugar rush would do him wonders.

"Hang in there, Henry. I'm coming, kid."

HENRY WAS HANGING IN THERE, LITERALLY, AS HE attempted to free himself from the plastic cuffs on his wrists. He'd spent hours rubbing the damn things against the edge of a door hinge and it had done him no good. The plastic was resilient and the metal of the hinge too smooth to cut through it.

That was when he got the idea to use the nail. There was a thick rusted nail embedded up high in the wall of the small shed. Although there was no light, the moon's glow was leaking through gaps in the ancient roof. One of those moonbeams was shining on the nail, that is, when it wasn't blocked by gathering rain clouds.

Henry's plan had been simple. Jump up with his arms raised above his head and make the plastic cuffs hook themselves on the nail. Maybe they couldn't be cut easily but the teeth of the ratcheting mechanism that tightened them could only bear so much stress. Henry was betting that his body weight would be too much and the teeth would strip and release the cuffs. Implementing the plan was not as easy as he had assumed it would be.

He scraped his knuckles against the nail on his first leap and made a long painful scratch along his right forearm with the fourth attempt. When he finally managed to hook himself onto the nail nothing happened. He hung there with his feet dangling free of the shed's dirt floor and felt the tendons in his shoulders scream from the stress. Just when he thought his shoulders were about to dislocate, the teeth of the cuff gave in from the pressure and Henry dropped to the floor.

His wrists, arms, and knuckles were bloody, and his shoulders were on fire, but his hands were free, although his ankles were still bound. After he rested for a minute, Henry took off his sneakers and began using his hands to force the second plastic tie over his right foot. The cuffs had been tightened around his pant leg and socks. Once it was slid lower there was slack in the band. It was enough and Henry managed to slip it off with a little effort. Now, he needed to get out of a locked shed.

That was the easy part, as Henry had already figured out how to do it. The shed he was in had several old gardening implements leaning up against one of its corners. One of those tools was a shovel with a broken handle and the shed had a dirt floor.

Henry began digging with the stubby tool. He was going to free Makayla and his grandmother, and this time he would succeed or die. He would not fail again.

18

NO MERCY

TANNER ARRIVED AT ARMSTRONG'S LATEST LOCATION
a few minutes after one a.m.

The place was similar to the other sites
Armstrong had been using but was surrounded by
more vacant land. In place of a garage, there was an
old barn. Tanner assumed that was where he would
find Makayla, and possibly Henry and Laura. A look
through a scope with night vision capability revealed
that the doors of the building had been locked from
the outside with the use of chains and padlocks.
Parked near the home was an RV with its engine off
and its interior dark.

Before he could free Henry and the others,
Tanner needed to eliminate anyone who could harm
them. As he suspected, there was little in the way of
security. Armstrong believed he was dead and the

threat ended. The man would soon find out he had been wrong.

The property had no fence, but two men walked a lazy patrol around the perimeter while carrying rifles. Tanner watched them spend a few minutes talking before heading in separate directions. He lay in wait among a clump of bushes as one of the men headed his way. When the man passed his position, Tanner eased up behind him and took him to the ground while clamping a hand over his mouth.

The guy's rifle skittered away on the dull winter grass as Tanner pressed a knife to his neck.

"Where can I find Armstrong?"

Tanner removed his hand so the man could answer. Before killing anyone, he had to be certain he was at the right location.

"The… the house. Armstrong is in the house with Gramps and the others."

"What about the girls?"

"They're in the barn."

"Is someone keeping an eye on them inside?"

"No way. It stinks in there. Am I under arrest?"

"No," Tanner said. "You're not under arrest." He clamped a hand over the man's mouth and shoved the knife in hard beneath the sentry's armpit several times. The blade sliced and punctured organs along with nicking the axillary artery. The man's struggles soon ceased.

Tanner rose from the ground, shouldered the rifle, and began walking the route the sentry had been on. There was a moon in the sky that was a sliver shy of being full along with drifting clouds to obscure it. When the other perimeter guard saw the silhouette of a man with a rifle coming toward him, he took it to be the sentry Tanner had just killed.

If he wondered why the man was rushing toward him as they grew closer, it didn't alarm him. He had remained calm right up until the moment Tanner's features became visible along with the flash of the blade coming toward him.

The moan he made as the steel sank into his chest was loud, but it likely went unheard by anyone inside the house. Tanner dragged the body out of sight and stayed still, listening. When he heard nothing that sounded like a cry of alarm or movement, he stood and headed for the house.

The drug he'd been injected with earlier was still in his system and he could tell that his reflexes weren't at their peak. Regardless of that, he no longer felt sluggish, so he was ready for whoever he would come across in the house.

On his way there he passed a shed that had been padlocked and chained like the barn. Tanner tapped on the door, hoping for a reply. When none came, he moved on. Had he wandered to the rear of the small structure he would have seen the loose dirt that was beside a hole. Henry had dug his way out and was seeking to find his grandmother and Makayla.

HENRY WAS AT THE REAR OF THE BARN. HE WAS USING the shovel again after finding the barn doors padlocked. Breaking a window would have been easy and also noisy. While the digging made noise, it wasn't a sound that carried very far if done in a slow and methodical manner.

His hands were raw and bloody, as the broken handle of the shovel was rough and hard to grip. The more his hands bled the slicker the handle became.

Henry was aware that he might be wasting his time. If the barn had a concrete floor, he would never be able to break through it. He didn't think that would be the case, or so he hoped. As he crawled inside the hole he'd made beneath the barn's wall, he began digging upward. He was hitting small stones but nothing that felt like a solid slab of concrete.

After several minutes of digging he felt the shovel's blade hit something hard and flat. A sense of despair was blossoming in his breast until he reached up and felt the surface of the object.

Rubber! It's just a rubber mat that someone must have laid over the dirt floor.

The thick black mats were laid down in pieces that interlocked. After digging a wider hole, Henry was able to remove a section and drag it out of the small pit he'd dug.

The sound of whispered voices could be heard as he climbed up inside the barn. Henry called out in a soft voice. He couldn't see anything as the windows were painted. What little moonlight could leak in through the cracks in the wooden walls would have to wait until the clouds passed. A scent of urine was in the air and it was cold inside the building.

"Grandma? Makayla?"

"Henry?" Laura said.

"It's me. Where are you?"

"We're over here, Henry," Makayla said. "Follow my voice."

"Who is that?" said someone else. "Oh God, please be a cop."

"I'm not a cop, but I'll get you all out of here," Henry said.

He fumbled along in the dark with his eyes adjusting enough so that he could make out the shape of the cages the girls and his grandmother were being kept in. When he reached them, Makayla's voice came from his left.

"Henry, over here."

Henry knelt beside her cage. The area stank of body odor and pee. When Henry realized he was gripping the thin metal bars of a dog cage, he felt anger welling up inside him.

"They've kept you locked up like an animal?"

Makayla's fingers found his through the bars and Henry gripped her hand. The moon shone slivers of light inside the building as the clouds allowed a momentary gap between them. Makayla's long hair was tangled, and her face appeared gaunt, her eyes hollow. Seeing the sad conditions his girlfriend had been forced to endure filled Henry with rage.

His grandmother called to him. She was in a cage near the back. After giving the fingers of Makayla's hand a squeeze of comfort, Henry went to his grandmother.

"How did you get free?"

"I got out of the cuffs and then dug my way out of the shed they locked me in."

"You can't free us by yourself. You need to go and find help, the police."

"I won't leave you and Makayla. I'll find something that will break the locks on your cages."

"No, Henry. Listen to me. Get yourself to safety first, then send help."

Henry shook his head vigorously. "I can't just leave you here."

"Your grandmother is right, Henry," Makayla said. "Leave and find a police officer, that way we'll know you're safe."

There was a blonde girl in a cage that sat between Makayla's enclosure and the one Henry's grandmother was locked in. When she opened her mouth, Henry thought she was doing so to give an opinion. She wasn't offering an opinion; she was betraying him and her fellow captives. She was the snitch that Gramps had cultivated. The girl screamed as loud as she could. It was a sound that carried well, and lights began coming on inside the house.

TANNER HAD MADE A CIRCUIT AROUND THE HOME. It told him that every window and door was locked. Given the late hour, it was likely that most of the people inside were asleep. And yet, it would only take one person who was awake and alert to ruin his plans to sneak inside.

He had to risk it, so he took out a set of lockpicks and went to work on a side door. He defeated the lock and was easing the door open when the scream pierced the quiet of the night. The sound of movement came from below as the remainder of Armstrong's men stirred awake.

The door Tanner had unlocked led to a landing. One set of stairs granted access down into the basement while the other shorter set ran up to another door that led into the kitchen. There was a soft humming sound coming from below as the electric heater warmed the basement, some of the warmth drifted upward and Tanner welcomed the feel of it on his chilled flesh.

As the men below rose from their beds, gruff voices asked each other what was going on as someone turned on a lamp.

"I heard a scream. It must be one of the girls."

Tanner eased the door shut behind him and crept up three wooden steps to stand by the kitchen door. He waited with his rifle aimed at the small landing below him. Throats were cleared, sleepy eyes were rubbed, and pants were pulled on as the men prepared to check on the disturbance.

When they were ready, the four men bounded up the stairs, and as the first man made the turn to head up into the kitchen, Tanner opened fire. More screams pierced the night as Tanner sent shot after shot into the white slavers. When all four men were down, Tanner changed magazines, then opened the kitchen door and began his search for Armstrong.

Armstrong heard the scream and recognized it for what it was, a signal. Unlike the other locations where they had kept the girls, the old barn hadn't been soundproofed. Gramps had told the girl who was spying for them to scream if anything serious was happening. She had done so.

Tanner? No, he's dead. He has to be dead.

Armstrong was slipping his feet inside his shoes when he heard Tanner open up on the men in the basement. They were muffled shots but the agonized grunts of pain they caused were explicit and loud.

Tanner or not, something had gone seriously wrong. Armstrong grabbed his gun and was about to open the door to his bedroom when he decided he needed to be more cautious. Moving over to the window, he unlocked it, then raised it to step out onto the roof that overhung the porch. He was relieved to see that there were no police lights flashing outside. After moving across the roof until he was at the side of the house, Armstrong stuck his gun in his waistband. He needed his hands free so he could lower himself over the roof's edge. He did so, then released his grip so that he could fall the short drop to the ground. After landing well on bent knees, Armstrong headed toward the barn. He needed to know what the hell was going on.

TANNER CAME ACROSS GRANNY AS HE REACHED THE top of the stairs leading up to the second floor. The old woman had been in the bathroom and was just leaving it. She was unarmed and holding a pink plastic container that held her dentures.

"Where's Armstrong?" Tanner asked.

Gramps came out of a room across the hall. He grabbed Granny by the hair and pulled her in front of him, to use as a shield. In his other hand he was holding an old Colt Detective Special; the stubby revolver had a nickel finish and a wooden grip.

Tanner blasted the pair as Gramps was raising his arm to fire. A total of six shots ripped through the old man, four of which had passed through the old woman first. Granny was not a hostage; she was a monster who had facilitated the abduction and degradation of an untold number of girls and young women. Tanner had no mercy for her.

He stepped over the still twitching forms of the dying septuagenarians and searched the rooms. When he came across the open window in Armstrong's bedroom, he realized that it had been used as a means of escape.

Confident that no one else was in the house, Tanner left through the home's front door and headed for the barn. As the clouds overhead parted, he could make out a figure undoing the locks on the barn door. It was a black man; his shaved scalp was gleaming beneath the moon's glow. Tanner was not going to reach him before he could enter the barn.

ARMSTRONG PULLED THE CHAIN FREE OF THE DOOR handles. He'd been glad to find the door still locked. Whatever else was going on, it appeared that no one had freed the girls. That was good, it meant that he could use them as hostages if needed.

"Armstrong?"

His name had been shouted from the direction of the house and had the intonation of a question. When he turned, he saw the dark shape of a man with a rifle running toward him.

"It's Tanner. Drop your weapon and I'll let you live."

Armstrong's answer was to dive inside the barn. Tanner had fired a shot on the fly. The slug buried itself in the wood where Armstrong's head had been. After landing inside the barn, Armstrong scrambled to his feet and slammed the door shut. Afterward he slid home a bolt to lock it.

"A boy broke in here," said a female voice. "It's why I screamed."

Armstrong felt for the light switch. When the overhead incandescent bulbs came on, he saw Henry standing near his grandmother's cage with a shovel in his hands.

"Tanner is out there, isn't he?" Henry said.

Armstrong was glaring at him with a confused

stare. "The door was locked. How the hell did you get in here?"

Henry pointed toward the hole he'd dug at the rear of the barn. "I tunneled in. Why don't you leave that way while you still can, before Tanner gets you."

Armstrong crouched low as he heard movement outside the door. Tanner had reached the barn. Using the girls as hostages might not work with a man like Tanner. Armstrong bolted for the hole at the rear of the barn. If he could crawl out before Tanner broke in, he could make it to his car and get away. The hell with the girls and the money they would bring. He couldn't spend it if he was dead.

He hit the ground and clawed his way into the hole. It was a tight fit, as Henry had fashioned it to accommodate his smaller frame. However, it proved to be wide enough. Armstrong was grinning when his head emerged out the other side and he saw no sign of Tanner.

TANNER WAS STILL AT THE FRONT OF THE BARN AND facing a dilemma. He couldn't risk firing through the walls at Armstrong for fear of hitting Henry or one of the girls. If he tried to enter through the door, he'd be an easy target to shoot at.

He was considering several options when he

heard a masculine scream come from the other side of the building. Whoever had made the sound was experiencing great pain.

Henry had waited until Armstrong was deep inside the hole before following him into it. The slaver of women had been lifting himself out of the other side when Henry drove the tip of the shovel's blade into Armstrong's back.

The metal broke through the fabric of Armstrong's shirt, entered his flesh, and cracked a rib. The scream the blow produced gave Henry pleasure. Armstrong was responsible for the horror he, Makayla, and his grandmother had experienced over the last few days. Henry thought the man couldn't suffer enough.

Armstrong's movements were tinged with panic as he slid himself the rest of the way out of the hole. Henry had made another thrust with the shovel, this time he caught Armstrong on the back of his left ankle, which severed the Achilles tendon. It elicited another scream from Armstrong. After climbing from the hole, he rolled over onto his back, panting.

As Henry scrambled out of the hole, Armstrong raised up his gun. Henry threw the shovel at him. It hit Armstrong in the face, ripping open a nostril and his upper lip. The shot Armstrong fired sailed over Henry's head.

He was out of the hole and leaping onto Armstrong before the man could fire off another round. Henry bit down hard on the hand holding the gun and the weapon was released. Henry was pounding blow upon blow on Armstrong's face when a knee was rammed against his groin. The pain and nausea that followed took the fight out of Henry.

Armstrong pushed the boy off, reclaimed his gun, and staggered to his feet. He was glaring down at Henry with a look of white-hot hatred as he slid his finger onto the trigger.

Three shots came from a corner of the barn and Armstrong spun around before falling. Tanner had shot him before he could kill Henry.

Armstrong lay on his back moaning from his injuries. One of the exit wounds in his chest was leaking blood by the pint.

Tanner stood over the dying man as he offered Henry a hand to stand up. The two of them watched in silence as Armstrong died.

19

VIGILANTE

TANNER NEVER ENTERED THE BARN, AND THUS, HE was never seen by Laura and the girls. They had heard Henry mention the name Tanner to Armstrong.

When the police and the FBI arrived on the property, they were told that there had been a disagreement between members of Armstrong's gang. Henry claimed that after his grandmother had been taken to the barn that he had witnessed a dispute between a man named Tanner and Armstrong.

Tanner told Armstrong that he had crossed a line by kidnapping Henry and his grandmother and that it would cause the authorities to double their efforts to locate them. Tanner wanted to let everyone go and start up the operation elsewhere.

"And what did this man Tanner look like?" Agent Croft asked Henry. The conversation took place in front of the barn while a paramedic was seeing to Henry's damaged hands.

Henry told Croft that the fictional Tanner wasn't a very tall man.

"He was about my height, but heavy, maybe around two twenty."

"Hair and eye color?"

"Sorta blond, with a beard that was darker."

"Any accent?"

"No—wait! Yeah, I think he might have been from the south from the way he talked. You know, like Mississippi or somewhere."

Henry went on to say that Tanner had two accomplices. After killing Armstrong and the others, they took a car and drove off. Henry had dug a set of keys out of Armstrong's pocket and freed his grandmother and the girls before entering the house to call the police.

Croft said that he would interview Henry further after he'd been given an examination at the hospital.

"I'm good, except for my hands and a headache."

"Did Armstrong say why he kidnapped you?"

"No. Maybe he wanted more hostages to trade in case he was caught."

"Maybe."

"The guy who took my grandmother and me also had my rifle, an M1 Garand. Have you seen it?"

"I haven't, but there are other weapons on the scene. They'll all be held as evidence and run through ballistics. About that rifle, did you use it at your house to kill the men who attacked you?"

"Yes. They broke in with guns."

"That must have been scary, and killing them was a hard thing to do, especially for someone as young as you. When we get to the hospital, I'll see if there's a therapist there you can talk to about it."

"I don't need to talk to anyone. Those guys got what they deserved."

Croft looked taken aback by Henry's attitude, then he winced at the lump on the back of Henry's head. "You still need to be looked at, just in case. And you're a hero, Henry. Even if that man Tanner hadn't betrayed his boss, you still would have escaped and called us."

Henry disagreed. "Armstrong had me. If Tanner hadn't shot him, I'd be dead. I failed again."

Croft tapped Henry on the chest with his notebook. "Don't be down on yourself; you're a hell of a kid."

LAURA HAD FARED BETTER THAN THE OTHER CAPTIVES because she'd only spent hours locked in a cage instead of days. The experience still terrified her. Makayla and the other girls had been rushed to the hospital, where they would reunite with their families.

Agent Croft had informed Laura about the destruction of her and Henry's home. That revelation brought tears to her eyes.

"We've got nowhere to go."

"What about friends?"

"Yes, I know someone who would put us up for a night or two, but I won't impose. I'll have to dip into my savings to get a motel room. Oh, this whole thing has been such a nightmare."

NIGHTMARES ARE WHAT MAKAYLA SUFFERED FROM IN the following days. She and the other girls would be receiving therapy to help them cope with the ordeal they'd been through. As bad as it was, without Tanner's interference they would have soon experienced greater horrors had they been sold. Henry met with Makayla in the hospital two days later. She had news.

"You're moving back to Italy?"

"Yes. My father asked if he could return to his

previous position and his company agreed. My grandfather also wants us to come home."

"Damn, Makayla. I ...I can't move to Italy."

"I know, Henry, and I don't want to go either, but my parents think it's for the best."

Henry took her hand. "Promise we'll stay in touch."

Makayla smiled. "Yes. We'll talk online every day, and maybe I'll be able to come back in the summer."

"Hey Makayla."

"Yes?"

"I'm so sorry I couldn't stop those guys from taking you."

"Are you serious? Henry, you were insane to fight them the way you did. I thought they had killed you."

"You don't blame me then?"

Makayla answered him with a kiss.

THE NEXT DAY, LAURA OPENED THE DOOR OF HER motel room after looking out the peephole. Cody and Sara smiled at her.

"Thanks for inviting us here," Cody said as they entered the room. "I've been wondering how Henry was doing."

"You've spoken to him on the phone."

"Yes, but it's not the same as seeing him in person."

"Henry will be here soon. The school bus drops him off at the curb. I wanted to speak to you alone first."

"I'm not surprised. Henry told me you were wondering why we came to see you the other day. He also said that you know what happened to Brock Kessler."

"He said that you were responsible for Kessler's disappearance. I want to thank you for that. I also want to know why you would do such a thing."

Cody was going to suggest that they sit down, but other than a single chair positioned near the closet there was nowhere to settle but on the side of the twin beds. Laura and Henry had lost everything in the fire and the hotel room was all she could afford until the insurance was paid.

"After my family was killed, I spent years learning how to defend myself, learning how to fight back. When we ran into Henry years ago and I saw what a threat Kessler was... I couldn't just walk away."

"And when Henry pleaded for help again, you came."

"Yes."

"Are you some sort of vigilante, Mr. Parker?"

"I would not categorize myself that way, no."

"Laura," Sara said. "Cody would never say this about himself, but yes, he helps people. I think he has helped more people over the years than he realizes. Because of what happened to his family, my husband will never stand by and see evil triumph, not when he knows he can do something about it."

Laura stared at them both, then held out her hand to Cody. "I want to thank you for avenging my daughter's death."

Cody shook her hand but said nothing. If she wanted details about Kessler's fate, she wasn't going to get them.

"We'd like to help you again," Sara said.

"In what way?"

"We have an offer for you, one we hope you'll accept."

Laura looked back and forth at the couple. "I'm listening."

Sara explained. "There's a vacant house on our ranch in Texas that's fully furnished. We'd like to offer it to you and Henry."

"You mean for free?"

"The home is just sitting there going unused."

"I won't accept it for free; I'd be willing to pay you a fair price to rent it."

"Does that mean you'll consider it?"

"Yes," Laura said.

Cody and Sara looked at each other. They hadn't

expected Laura to agree so swiftly. She read their expressions correctly and smiled.

"You're wondering why I would agree to move to Texas so fast, yes?"

"You did seem to make a decision rather quickly," Sara said.

"Henry and I have no other family here and with our home being destroyed and all we've been through, a change sounds like a good idea. I was planning on selling the house anyway and with Makayla moving away, Henry won't mind leaving the area. He's somewhat of a loner, as am I."

Cody was staring at Laura. "There's something else, isn't there? Another reason?"

"You're perceptive, Mr. Parker. It's Henry's father. I... I don't want to discuss the man except to say that he's dangerous. There's been no contact from him since just after Henry was born and for years I hoped that meant he was dead. Henry has been on the news and there's a possibility his father might have seen him on TV and want to make contact. If we leave the area it will make it difficult for that to happen."

"Henry told me that the FBI is interested in his father. Why is that?" Cody asked.

"The man is a criminal who escaped justice. I don't want to say any more than that."

"We won't pry," Sara said.

"Thank you for understanding. I find talking about Henry's father to be difficult. That man hurt my daughter and I… thank you."

The school bus arrived, and Henry got off wearing a backpack. He shuffled along looking depressed. In the last few days he had lost his home and his girlfriend. When he entered the motel room and saw Cody and Sara, he smiled and hugged them both.

Laura tousled his hair. "Hey, kiddo. I have news that might cheer you up."

20

I WANT TO BE YOU

Laura and Henry arrived at the ranch three weeks later.

The insurance company paid Laura's claim for the fire, but once she was done repaying the money owed on the property there wasn't very much left. Glenn had eaten up what little equity they'd built by taking out a loan to gamble with.

Sara had convinced Laura that she and Henry needed a fresh start. By moving to Texas and renting the other home on their property, things would certainly be different for them.

Steve Mendez agreed to hire Laura for the job of police dispatcher as a favor to Cody. The home Laura and Henry would be living in, the old Kinney place, was fully furnished, saving Laura the need to buy furniture.

Stark had a good public school system and motocross racing was big in the area, so Henry could continue in his sport.

HENRY HAD NEVER RIDDEN A HORSE, BUT HE TOOK TO it well. After he'd been there for a week he was riding along with Cody and looking at ease in the saddle.

"Makayla was supposed to call me yesterday but didn't. When I finally reached her, she admitted she had been out on a date with her old boyfriend."

"At least she didn't lie," Cody said.

"I can't blame her. I mean, we're separated by over five thousand miles and have no idea when we'll see each other again. That doesn't mean I don't still love her."

"You might get together again someday. Life can be surprising."

"Were you ever serious with anyone before you met Sara?"

"Yeah."

"What happened?"

"Let's just say that I was even more unlucky in love than you were."

"Oh."

"Yeah."

Before heading back to the stables, Cody decided to ride out to the front of their property and see if there was any mail. It was one of those normal parts of life that he never had to consider when he'd been living the nomadic off-grid life of Tanner. As a kid growing up on the ranch, grabbing the mail had been one of his chores. It sometimes made him feel nostalgic when he did it.

As he leaned down to look inside the box, a blue SUV slowed and parked a short distance away. The driver was Caroline Lang, the mother of the little boy Cody had found wandering. Little Jarod was fastened into a car seat. He appeared to be asleep. Caroline had another passenger. She was a girl with long blonde hair who was Henry's age.

Caroline and the girl left their vehicle and walked up to Cody.

"Hi, Mr. Parker. I was driving by and saw you. I wanted to stop and thank you again for what you did for Jarod."

"As I said, I'm glad I could help. And call me Cody, we're neighbors."

Caroline smiled. "And I'm Caroline. By the way, this is my little sister, Olivia."

Olivia was smiling, but not at Cody, she was grinning up at Henry, who was smiling back at her. Cody introduced Henry and mentioned that he was also a neighbor.

"I heard there was a new kid in school," Olivia said.

"That would be me," Henry admitted, from where he sat atop his horse.

Caroline said she had to run home and make dinner.

"It's been nice seeing you again Mr.... I mean Cody. And it was a pleasure to meet you, Henry."

"Same here," Henry said, but he was looking at Olivia.

As their vehicle drove away, Cody glanced over at Henry.

"Maybe you and Olivia could help each other with homework sometimes."

Henry smiled. "I might mention that to her the next time I see her."

Cody grabbed the mail. It was all bills and credit card offers. He stuffed them into an inside pocket of his jacket and bade his horse to turn around for the ride to the stables.

"Grandma still won't tell me about my father."

"Did she say why?"

"The same old thing; she doesn't think I'm old enough to hear the truth. I told her I was old enough to kill two men and she said not to mention that either."

"About killing those men, did it upset you?"

"Hell no. Those scumbags got what they deserved."

Cody nodded. "I'm told it bothers most people; I've never been one of them."

"How old were you when you killed for the first time?"

"Sixteen. They were trying to abduct my stepmother, Claire. I killed all three of them."

They reached the stables and loosened the cinches on their horses. After taking off the tack, they offered the horses water, then put them in their stalls.

"We'll take a longer ride soon; I think you're ready for it," Cody said.

"Will you train me? I mean teach me to fight?"

"Like boxing?"

"No, everything. I want to be like you, Cody. I want to be a Tanner someday."

"Do you know what you're asking? I'm a trained killer, Henry. I murder people. That's what I do. I know you've killed in self-defense but what I do is different, it's also illegal and dangerous."

"I get that, I do, but it's what I want. I don't ever want to feel helpless again."

Cody shook his head. "You're too young."

"Oh God, you too? I'm not a damn baby."

Cody reached out and gave Henry's shoulder a

squeeze. "You're too young to train as a Tanner; that doesn't mean I'm saying no."

"So, you'll train me?"

"I'll teach you how to fight and instruct you on how to use certain weapons, *if* your grandmother says it's okay."

"She will. She gave up on trying to keep my rifle away from me a long time ago. What about me becoming a Tanner?"

Cody held up a hand. "When you're a little older, say seventeen or eighteen, we'll see if you still want it. Believe me, you have to really want it to become one."

Henry broke eye contact. "I've wanted to be like you ever since we first met. I used to think that meant I had to become a secret agent."

"Agent X."

Henry looked up. "Yeah, Agent X." Something occurred to Henry then and a look of alarm entered his eyes. "You're not training anyone else, are you?"

"No, and I hope to name a Tanner Eight someday."

Henry grinned. "You're looking at him. I won't just wait until I'm older. I'll start training now. What are some of the things I can do?"

"Like my mentor Tanner Six, I speak more than one language. Being able to do so comes in handy, and it's saved my life at times."

"Learn a new language? I can do that. What else?"

Cody ruffled Henry's hair. "For now, just enjoy being a kid. It's something we only get one chance at."

As they left the stables, Henry sighed. "I miss Makayla."

"Yeah, but that girl Olivia seemed to like you."

"You think?"

"I do."

"Hey, Cody?"

"Yes?"

"Thanks for letting Grandma and I move here."

"It was Sara's idea, but I agreed."

"Man, I can't wait to grow up."

"Most people feel that way at fifteen. At forty, you wish you could go back."

"You'd want to be my age again? Why?"

"I didn't know how good I had it."

"You're talking about your family, but now you and Sara have a family."

"Life has given me a second chance at being Cody Parker."

"No offense, dude, but being Tanner is way cooler."

Cody grinned. "I can't argue with that."

TANNER RETURNS!

PROTECTOR - BOOK 30

AFTERWORD

Thank you,

REMINGTON KANE

JOIN MY INNER CIRCLE

You'll receive FREE books, such as,

SLAY BELLS – A TANNER NOVEL – BOOK 0

TAKEN! ALPHABET SERIES – 26 ORIGINAL TAKEN! TALES

BLUE STEELE - KARMA

Also – Exclusive short stories featuring TANNER, along with other books.

TO BECOME AN INNER CIRCLE MEMBER, GO TO:
   http://remingtonkane.com/mailing-list/

ALSO BY REMINGTON KANE

The TANNER Series in order

INEVITABLE I - A Tanner Novel - Book 1

KILL IN PLAIN SIGHT - A Tanner Novel - Book 2

MAKING A KILLING ON WALL STREET - A Tanner Novel - Book 3

THE FIRST ONE TO DIE LOSES - A Tanner Novel - Book 4

THE LIFE & DEATH OF CODY PARKER - A Tanner Novel - Book 5

WAR - A Tanner Novel- A Tanner Novel - Book 6

SUICIDE OR DEATH - A Tanner Novel - Book 7

TWO FOR THE KILL - A Tanner Novel - Book 8

BALLET OF DEATH - A Tanner Novel - Book 9

MORE DANGEROUS THAN MAN - A Tanner Novel - Book 10

TANNER TIMES TWO - A Tanner Novel - Book 11

OCCUPATION: DEATH - A Tanner Novel - Book 12

HELL FOR HIRE - A Tanner Novel - Book 13

A HOME TO DIE FOR - A Tanner Novel - Book 14

FIRE WITH FIRE - A Tanner Novel - Book 15

MISSING - A Tanner Novel - Book 37

CONTENDER - A Tanner Novel - Book 38

TO SERVE AND PROTECT - A Tanner Novel - Book 39

STALKING HORSE - A Tanner Novel - Book 40

THE EVIL OF TWO LESSERS - A Tanner Novel - Book 41

SINS OF THE FATHER AND MOTHER - A Tanner Novel - Book 42

SOULLESS - A Tanner Novel - Book 43

The Young Guns Series in order

YOUNG GUNS

YOUNG GUNS 2 - SMOKE & MIRRORS

YOUNG GUNS 3 - BEYOND LIMITS

YOUNG GUNS 4 - RYKER'S RAIDERS

YOUNG GUNS 5 - ULTIMATE TRAINING

YOUNG GUNS 6 - CONTRACT TO KILL

YOUNG GUNS 7 - FIRST LOVE

YOUNG GUNS 8 - THE END OF THE BEGINNING

A Tanner Series in order

TANNER: YEAR ONE

TANNER: YEAR TWO

TANNER: YEAR THREE

TANNER: YEAR FOUR

TANNER: YEAR FIVE

The TAKEN! Series in order

TAKEN! - LOVE CONQUERS ALL - Book 1

TAKEN! - SECRETS & LIES - Book 2

TAKEN! - STALKER - Book 3

TAKEN! - BREAKOUT! - Book 4

TAKEN! - THE THIRTY-NINE - Book 5

TAKEN! - KIDNAPPING THE DEVIL - Book 6

TAKEN! - HIT SQUAD - Book 7

TAKEN! - MASQUERADE - Book 8

TAKEN! - SERIOUS BUSINESS - Book 9

TAKEN! - THE COUPLE THAT SLAYS TOGETHER - Book 10

TAKEN! - PUT ASUNDER - Book 11

TAKEN! - LIKE BOND, ONLY BETTER - Book 12

TAKEN! - MEDIEVAL - Book 13

TAKEN! - RISEN! - Book 14

TAKEN! - VACATION - Book 15

TAKEN! - MICHAEL - Book 16

TAKEN! - BEDEVILED - Book 17

TAKEN! - INTENTIONAL ACTS OF VIOLENCE - Book 18

TAKEN! - THE KING OF KILLERS – Book 19

TAKEN! - NO MORE MR. NICE GUY - Book 20 & the Series Finale

The MR. WHITE Series

PAST IMPERFECT - MR. WHITE - Book 1

HUNTED - MR. WHITE - Book 2

The BLUE STEELE Series in order

BLUE STEELE - BOUNTY HUNTER- Book 1

BLUE STEELE - BROKEN- Book 2

BLUE STEELE - VENGEANCE- Book 3

BLUE STEELE - THAT WHICH DOESN'T KILL ME- Book 4

BLUE STEELE - ON THE HUNT- Book 5

BLUE STEELE - PAST SINS - Book 6

BLUE STEELE - DADDY'S GIRL - Book 7 & the Series Finale

The CALIBER DETECTIVE AGENCY Series in order

CALIBER DETECTIVE AGENCY - GENERATIONS- Book 1

CALIBER DETECTIVE AGENCY - TEMPTATION-
Book 2

CALIBER DETECTIVE AGENCY - A RANSOM PAID
IN BLOOD- Book 3

CALIBER DETECTIVE AGENCY - MISSING- Book 4

CALIBER DETECTIVE AGENCY - DECEPTION-
Book 5

CALIBER DETECTIVE AGENCY - CRUCIBLE- Book 6

CALIBER DETECTIVE AGENCY – LEGENDARY –
Book 7

CALIBER DETECTIVE AGENCY – WE ARE
GATHERED HERE TODAY - Book 8

CALIBER DETECTIVE AGENCY - MEANS, MOTIVE,
and OPPORTUNITY - Book 9 & the Series Finale

THE TAKEN!/TANNER Series in order

THE CONTRACT: KILL JESSICA WHITE -
Taken!/Tanner - Book 1

UNFINISHED BUSINESS – Taken!/Tanner – Book 2

THE ABDUCTION OF THOMAS LAWSON -
Taken!/Tanner – Book 3

PREDATOR - Taken!/Tanner - Book 4

DETECTIVE PIERCE Series in order

MONSTERS - A Detective Pierce Novel - Book 1

DEMONS - A Detective Pierce Novel - Book 2

ANGELS - A Detective Pierce Novel - Book 3

THE OCEAN BEACH ISLAND Series in order

THE MANY AND THE ONE - Book 1

SINS & SECOND CHANES - Book 2

DRY ADULTERY, WET AMBITION -Book 3

OF TONGUE AND PEN - Book 4

ALL GOOD THINGS… - Book 5

LITTLE WHITE SINS - Book 6

THE LIGHT OF DARKNESS - Book 7

STERN ISLAND - Book 8 & the Series Finale

THE REVENGE Series in order

JOHNNY REVENGE - The Revenge Series - Book 1

THE APPOINTMENT KILLER - The Revenge Series -
Book 2

AN I FOR AN I - The Revenge Series - Book 3

ALSO

THE EFFECT: Reality is changing!

THE FIX-IT MAN: A Tale of True Love and Revenge

DOUBLE OR NOTHING

PARKER & KNIGHT

REDEMPTION: Someone's taken her

DESOLATION LAKE

TIME TRAVEL TALES & OTHER SHORT STORIES

Made in the USA
Coppell, TX
29 April 2022